DONUT ENTER

A PENNY LANE BOOK CLUB MYSTERY
BOOK 2

MARY ANN TIPPETT

MAT BOOKS

"When the skillet seethes, and a blubber hot
Tilts the lid of the coffee-pot,
And the scent of the buckwheat cake grows plain —
O then is the time for a brave refrain."
— James Whitcomb Riley

PROLOGUE

I refrain from another turn around Holstein House and rest on the wicker chair that, as always, cannot creak from the weight I lack.

I never knew boredom as a touring performer. Now I have only these halls, my last residence, to haunt. Cursed to drag my spirit from room to room, I dwell not on lost love. In the end, my useless arm, thanks to the first stroke, tormented me most. And now, I've no audience to amuse with my orations.

Trapped within these walls, I attempt to block the maddening din beyond the gates. A thick canopy of trees on the grounds has dwindled to a measly few. My home now serves as a museum, with an almost daily encroaching public. These distractions rob me of inspiration. Just as my paralyzed arm yielded no pleasure for this poet who could no longer write. And yet...

There is hope. A studious young woman called Daisy, who occupied the security desk tonight, scurried off moments ago. She heard me though. I am sure of it.

I was reciting an ode to Clara, working out lines and

rhymes as I paced the great hall from living room to library. Daisy alerted after resting her head on a stack of books. Curious, I paused my monologue. In that brief silence, her eyes flew open and stared straight into mine.

This phenomenon feels more exciting than what happened with the vase, when I first discovered my ability to bend objects to my will. It was a cheap vessel, thoughtlessly placed on my bureau alongside my mother's portrait. I lost my temper, stormed about the room, and swiped at the offensive object. My arm made contact, causing that modern eyesore to fall into pieces on the floor. Spiritual angst, it seems, collides with the laws of physics during times of fury.

I have another ability, less satisfying. I can smell things. Although I cannot chew, taste or consume comestibles, I smell them. Youngsters with totes are the biggest invokers of this torment. Tuna sandwiches, ginger cookies, and overripe bananas are but a few of the intense aromas I sense on this side of the ether. Some are more tolerable than others, but what causes me the most nostalgic suffering are the cakes.

My mother made fried buckwheat cakes on special occasions. Donuts is the modern version. Lately, these round little memory provokers accost me regularly. They come tucked into brown paper bags or stacked into boxes and are served on picnic tables.

At first, their sugary scent produced waves of grief, reminding me of all I lost when the second stroke finished me. Then the grief turned to anger. How have I earned this torture? Why cannot my spirit rest in peace?

However, I digress.

Tonight, a new supernatural ability revealed itself, this one more interesting than the others. Before, no living person acknowledged my presence. Daisy did. She started awake and locked eyes with me.

What can it mean? Why would anyone suddenly see me? Does she hold the key to my release? Has she opened a door through which I might exit a world no longer meant for me?

She was gone in a flash, leaving me alone to brood on my memories, my mother's festive cakes chief among them. The memory is so potent I can almost taste it.

Now I hear footsteps. The donut aroma is back. Who is this intruder breaching the sanctuary of my study with his deafening steps and buttery odour?

I rise from my chair, barely noticing the wicker's creak. There, at the top of the stairs outside my bedroom, stands the offender. He crams what remains of the snack into his mouth with appalling rudeness. What audacity, to not even pause; sit at a table and savour the luxury of taste.

A flash of fury courses through me. I want nothing more than relief from this sentient affliction, this accosting sensation, this invasive madness. It is too much to bear.

ONE

When Paula opened The Penny Lane Book Club to new members, she expected less than ten at the planning meeting. "People are flaky, Daisy," my mother explained. "One minute they are gung ho about one cause or another and the very next minute it's forgotten." When I reminded her our stick house parlour barely sat five people, she said, "People can stand. It won't take long." She and Rita, an original book club member, had developed an efficient agenda: members would make a swift decision on publicity, theme and venue. Short and sweet. Paula flicked the piece of paper at me, its agenda items glaringly succinct, to emphasize her point.

Now half of Lockerbie flattened the brittle grass outside our cramped little home. We stood shoulder to shoulder as the last leaves floated from the oak between our yard and the Marshalls' next door. A sliver of sunlight disappeared inside a slate sheath of clouds as I fought the impulse to sneak away and find a sweater.

Paula's clipboard shook in her hand as she stamped a foot on our tiny porch. "Right then," she said, eyeing the crowd that clearly would not fit inside the house. She drew a line through one of her agenda items. "No need to discuss publicity."

Petra, my best friend and fellow deserter of the original book club, elbowed me. "That was a warm welcome," she whispered, not bothering to mask her sarcasm. She had misgivings about Paula's social skills.

Stan raised his hand. "Actually, I have some ideas about publicity," he shouted over the yelp of a dog wriggling in someone's arms.

I stood on tiptoe to see. Stan was at the front of the crowd, bouncing to keep warm. "Everyone is in short sleeves," I whispered to Petra. "I tried to warn her we wouldn't all fit inside."

Stan was especially keen to join the book club. He had stopped me countless times on my way past his house to enthuse about one aspect of book clubbing or another. What books would we discuss? He wanted to know. Where would we hold the discussions? Who else was joining? When could he meet the other members? Between law school, filling in for Mom at the museum, and being a thorn in Jenny's side at the hair salon where I worked, I had no time for these questions. I kept telling him to ask Paula and Rita, which only invited more questions.

Stan's interruption rattled Paula. "Ideas about publicity?" she asked, her voice wavering. I knew she was tempted to side-step Stan's remark; to redirect everyone to the next topic. But she had learned from past mistakes. The old book club unraveled, in part, because of her single-minded opinions. She wanted this book club to be different. She would strive for cohesion or die trying. Pressing her mouth toward one cheek, then the other, she attempted an air of openness.

"Yes," Stan answered. "Pinning notices to telephone poles, for example." He clutched his bowling bag close to his chest. "I made flyers. We just need to figure out the schedule and," he glanced at the crowd behind him that overwhelmed our front yard, "location."

"I love your enthusiasm," Paula trilled, nodding repeatedly while she considered his comments. "Speaking of the schedule," she began, her eyes back on to the agenda.

"I can do a blog," our next door neighbour interrupted. The signature screech of Karen's voice came from behind the tree. "We have one at the neighbourhood association, where I serve as chief editor."

"A blog. Oh, my." Paula tightened her hands on her clipboard as if it was the last life vest on a sinking ship.

Poor Mom. Someone needed to throw her a lifeline. "Let's hear what Paula has to say," I shouted over the dog whining at the garbage truck clattering on the street. I nudged my way over to Karen's porch to redirect the crowd's attention. "She has an agenda to work through," I continued. "And she really wants us all to feel included in the planning of The Penny Lane Book Club's relaunch." My throat tightened, remembering how the original book club lacked an air of inclusiveness. Coughing through the tension, I continued. "We need to keep this meeting as focused and productive as possible so we can have an actual book club meeting. Which will hopefully be warmer."

Other than a few giggles, the crowd fell silent. Miraculously, the garbage truck rumbled away, and the dog settled.

"Thank you, Daisy," Paula said as all eyes turned back to her.

Next item on the list was venue. Given the size of the crowd, we agreed to assemble next at the community center. Rita would assess cost and availability. Stan would keep notes from the meetings and Karen would compile the information into a newsletter and email next steps to the group.

When Petra asked her about the discussion format, Paula tasked her with providing a survey for Karen to distribute. Rita would forward her notes on moderating, book selection, and refreshment options to Petra. We decided to hold one meeting per month on Sunday afternoon. Much to Stan's dismay, publicity was tabled until a large enough venue that complies with fire code regulations could be secured.

As the crowd shivered and clouds gathered, Paula introduced the last agenda item: tone and theme. "Shall we focus on one genre, for example, or permit a genre free-for-all?" I cringed at her choice of words, which clearly betrayed her preference. "Shall we organize books and refreshments around a different theme each month, or take a more casual approach for assembly?"

Stan's hand shot up. "I think we should have a purpose for gathering." He held up a wooden spire. "Most of us live in older houses that are in various stages of disrepair. What if our club raised funds and awareness for the Historical Society — a preservation focused theme, if you will."

"What about those of us who rent?" Petra countered. "I love Lockerbie as much as anyone, but why not focus on women's shelters? Homeless housing? Something less self serving."

Just then, the dog, having zoned in on a squirrel, darted to the oak, leaping and yipping as the squirrel taunted from a low branch. A toddler that Karen had been redirecting from her garden most of the meeting started wailing and writhing in his mother's arms. The crowd parted around her as the mother hurried away. The wind kicked up out of nowhere, producing a howl over which we couldn't hear each other.

As the chaos crescendoed, Martin the mailman handed me a letter. "Here's something for you, Daisy," he said with a wink, before marching to the next house. The crowd disbursed. Clutching the envelope, I glanced at our porch and noticed Paula hightailing it inside.

"Hell is other people," Petra mumbled.

"That is definitely Sarte," I accused. She loved to quote the most depressing philosophers.

She didn't bother to reply. Paula had overloaded Petra with more responsibility than she had time for. Her misery was understandable.

The letter in my hand had a familiar name typed in the corner. Farley Shian. My ex-boyfriend. My eyes met Petra's, wide with alarm. She knew all about my history with Farley.

"Come with me," she said.

I READ the letter aloud while she kneaded dough, chopped chocolate and managed one of her philosophy students who was serving customers. When I finished, I took a sip from the latte she handed me. The aroma from the apple scones she was baking gave me pie-a-la-mode vibes.

The gist of the letter was simple. Farley wanted to inform me about his move to Lockerbie. "This is just a heads up," he wrote. "To spare any awkwardness, you might feel bumping into me." He had moved on. He assumed I had as well. We could be adults about this, he reasoned.

"So?" Petra placed a tray of warm scones on a cooling rack, jolting me from a reverie of mixed emotions. "Is he right? Have you moved on?"

I knew what she meant. She liked to zone in on my relationship with Brett. Officer Harnette and I met during Jolee's murder investigation. Our connection was instant and intense. Although we dated as often as possible, we had no surplus of time given his police duties and my law school studies and two part-time jobs. We were miles from a *define the relationship* stage of dating.

"Define 'moved on,'" I stalled.

Petra's lips formed a straight, thin line. "If you have to ask, you probably haven't moved on."

Ouch. The sting not only hurt, it felt wrong. Whenever I thought of Brett, my stomach did a little flip. I had no such flip when I thought about Farley. But had we moved on? We never had a breakup conversation. He simply stayed in Bloomington, where he worked for his family's donut company. I focused on law school and hair styling. Months went by. Eventually, my family and friends stopped asking about him.

"I should not be surprised," I said, changing the subject. "Dixie Donuts opened a store here. I figured he would, I don't know, come to the grand opening or whatever."

Petra scowled. "Yeah, about that." She settled onto the stool next to me. "My scone business is not exactly thriving since they (she refused to say Dixie or Donuts) rolled into town."

"Oh, Petra. Everyone knows your scones and lattes are the best in town. It's just a blip. Sales will pick up. Right?" I covered her hand with mine, attempting to comfort her. How do you comfort someone whose dreams are crumbling though? Guilt stabbed at my insides. One stab for every time I could not walk past Dixie's without buying a donut.

Petra put her other hand on mine and squeezed.

"Thanks. I'll figure something out." She sprung up to pull a pan of dough from the refrigerator.

"Like what?" I watched, with mild alarm, as Petra added blue and yellow food colouring to the dough and blended the concoction in a giant food processor. I had never seen her put additives into her baked goods.

"Maybe pay someone to kill someone?" Petra joked. When I didn't react, she glanced at me, registering my surprise. "Don't judge," she said, "the matcha powder isn't green enough. I have to help it along or the scones turn out the colour of pond scum."

"Says the woman judging my ex for being disingenuous," I said, with no attempt to hide my smirk.

She squinted her eyes at me but did not take the bait. "Why now?" she said, back onto the letter subject. "Why must Farley preface his royal arrival with an air of finality? He could just say it in person when you *bump into him*." Puffs of green powder flew from her fingers as she made air quotes.

"Whatever," I deflected. "It must please you that the book club will be next door. More traffic for Petra's Pastries."

"If the community center has a room available that day." She patted at the green heap on the table in front of her, molding pieces of it into circles. "Besides, Dixies is open on Sundays as well." She sliced into the circles, creating a dozen plump triangles.

I felt another pang of guilt. When was the last time I bought a scone from Petra? I should be more supportive.

Aside from being a traitor to my best friend, something else bothered me. "I wonder why he typed the letter," I mused. He took pride in his artful penmanship.

Petra shrugged. "He's busy. No one writes in longhand anymore."

"Not even on the envelopes?" I stared hard at the address, especially the words "Miss Daisy McCartney" in type print. No matter how we parted, the cold tone felt off.

"Probably made his secretary do it," Petra said, wiping her hands on her apron. "Give me the letter." She crossed the kitchen and held her hand out.

Instinctively, I clutched the letter to my chest. "What are you going to do with it?"

Petra plopped down onto the stool next to me, our knees inches apart. "Daisy, if you want to enjoy whatever it is you have going with Officer Swooney-Pants, you need to let this go. Holding onto a thoughtless letter so you can over-analyze it is counterproductive."

She was right, and yet I felt my fingers tighten around the letter.

"Can I tell you something?" Her voice softened as I nodded. "You are too sensitive for law and too restless for hairstyling. Just my opinion, but I know you will figure it out. This thing you have with Brett is real. He's good to you." She rolled her eyes. "Clearly you adore each other." My grip loosened as she took the letter. "Don't waste your time on this."

Petra was my shoulder to cry on for months following Jolee's death. She was philosophical and wise. If she thought the letter would ruin the good thing I had with Brett, I had to let it go. For real.

So, like a woman who would eventually find her place in the world, I bought a butterscotch latte, an apple pie scone, and headed home to study, banishing all thoughts of the letter and its sender from my mind.

TWO

I shimmied past the perpetual line at the Dixie Donuts counter, scanning the dining area. Brett and two steaming cups of coffee waited at the corner booth. From across the dining area, I could see his jaw drop. Inwardly, I high fived myself for the salon chic outfit I chose. At Jolee's... I mean Jenny's...Hair Salon, we were required to dress in black. Today I wore skinny jeans and a sequined off-shoulder sweater.

"You look great," Brett said, popping out of his seat to kiss my cheek. His lips left behind a spark, which set off little brush fires up and down my neck. He must have noticed my cheeks pinken because he winked as he sat down. "Coffee is strong, but at least it's hot," he added, fixating his java eyes on my bare shoulder.

I slid into the booth across from him and wrapped my hands around the cup. "Thank you." His intense stare set my insides aflame. "There is nothing more attractive than a man in uniform bearing coffee," I said, wishing I could think of something wittier to say. A glint in his eye, a wink, a wonky smile. Everything he did made me fumble for words, it seemed. Even his text that morning, asking if I had time for coffee, made my toes curl and my tongue-tie. "Thanks for the invite. Everything okay?"

He reached for my hand, weaving his fingers through mine. I tried not to notice the fabric of his shirt tighten around bulging biceps. "It is now," he said, flashing one of those goofy Ryan Reynolds grins that turn my insides to goo. I swear he and Ryan are distant cousins. "I know you have to get to work soon." He signalled the server with his other hand. "Do you know what you want?"

Yes, I knew what I wanted. I wanted to stay right where I was all day, mooning over that grin. But he was right. Jenny wouldn't be impressed if I were late. One thing I learned since she took over the salon is that her sister got all the big-heartedness, with none to spare for her twin.

I dragged my eyes away from Brett and studied the list of flavours posted on the wall above the counter. "Butter-scotch glazed chocolate? Yes, please," I enthused. "Salted caramel peanut butter? Don't mind if I do. Lemon meringue! Oh goodness, I can't decide." The choices addled my brain.

Before I could decide, a server swooped over with a coffeepot. Her blond hair was parted in the middle and pulled into knobs above each ear. I had seen similar styles in some of the hair magazines we kept at the salon, but none were as whimsical. I made a mental note to check the newer issues. Had I missed the latest style?

"Hi, I'm Sadie," she said. There was a singsong lilt to her voice that, combined with the hairdo, mesmerized me.

Brett asked her about popular flavours. Still transfixed by her hair, I caught nothing from the conversation. My eyes ping-ponged from one pony tail nub to the other, like all my brain cells were caught up trying to decide where to focus my gaze.

"How does that sound, Daisy?" Brett's voice snapped me out of my little trance. "Absolutely." I took in a quick raspy breath, as if I'd just awakened from a nap. "I'll have what he's having."

"Are you okay?" Brett asked after Sadie left.

Did I mention I often stumble over words around Brett? So far, he hadn't caught on and I hoped to ditch the awkward behaviour as I got to know him better. "Yes, sorry." I jostled myself straighter. "So many choices!" I enthused, hoping whatever I ordered was something chocolate with maple or caramel influenced.

Brett tilted his head, scrutinizing me. I felt sorry for any suspect subjected to a lie detector test in his presence. Squirming, I gave him an all teeth no confidence smile. He relaxed those laser lie detector beams, finally, and changed the subject.

"Okay. So I work today, but I have tomorrow off. How about I wine and dine you at my place?" He winked as he brought the coffee cup to his soft lips, a simple act that made me squirm again. The good kind of squirm. The feeling-some-heat-under-my seat kind of squirm.

"Oh. That s-sounds nice," I stammered, over-delivering my return wink with a something-in-my-eye type squint. Awkward. A date with Brett was just what I needed to forget the letter from what's his name. Something to look forward to rather than backwards. Then I remembered I wasn't free tomorrow night. "Oh doodle-sticks, I work at the museum. I am free tonight, though. Perhaps a late snack after work?"

He shook his head, killing my hopes and dreams. "It's going to be a late one at the station."

"Two mango margarita donuts with pistachio glaze," Sadie said, plopping two plates down in front of us. What was with those knobs? Her head bobbing into view had my eyes all out of kilter again.

"Oh," I said. "Interesting choice." By interesting, I meant yuck. Mango margarita? Really?

Sadie shrugged and moved to a table of men in business suits waiting to order. Brett crammed half of a donut into his mouth, revealing orange covered teeth as he tried to flash a smile my way. "You sure you want yours?" he asked, his hand already reaching for my plate.

I did not want mine. Not at all. I also didn't want to admit to zoning out during some pivotal decision making. "Yes, hands off," I said, smacking his hand away.

He puckered his adorable mouth into a pout. Then he gave me the doe eyes.

"Fine. I'll save you a bite," I offered.

Brett's phone buzzed. He studied the incoming text. I took a nibble of the donut. I have to admit, the citrus and agave infusion dazzled my tongue. Still, I lean more toward comfort flavours like caramel, peanut butter and chocolate. Speaking of enticing brown things, Brett's eyes were dragging his brows toward each other. Uh oh. "What's wrong?" I asked.

"I'm sorry Daise. I have to head to the station." He pulled out some bills to leave on the table and crammed the last bite of donut into his mouth. "I'll see you soon, okay?"

His nickname for me was a little too dazed-and-confused sounding, but I registered with no small amount of tingling that we had reached the endearments stage of dating. Admiring his well-formed glutes as he left, I thought soon couldn't come soon enough.

"All set?" Sadie, with the duelling hair nobs, cleared our

plates and stuffed the cash into her pocket. She wore an apron as orange as the donuts, with lavender polka dots that reminded me of Jolee. I still thought about her every day. Working for her twin sister made her even harder to forget.

"Yes, thank you. It was nice to meet you, Sadie." I smiled, taking in her hair once more. The look was growing on me. Something about Sadie's yoga instructor voice and quirky hair set me at ease. "I'm Daisy, by the way. How is business? Do you enjoy working here?"

"Oh yes. I've worked for Dixie Corp awhile now. When the owners asked me to manage the Lockerbie store, I didn't hesitate. Great people to work for," she said.

Bloomington is a small town. I wondered if she knew Farley. I preferred to associate Dixie Donuts with Sadie, though, not my ex. He was dead to me. "That's great," I said. "Congratulations!"

"Thank you. Hold on a sec." She scooped a couple more plates from a table on her way to the kitchen. I glanced at my phone, realizing I had just enough time to get to Jenny's Salon if I started now.

Sadie intercepted me as I navigated around the takeout line to the door. "Here," she said, handing me a white paper bag with the Dixie logo printed on it. "I sensed you are more of a chocolate than a fruity donut person." God love her.

The donuts were still warm. "Wow, thank you!" She bowed her head quickly, namaste-style. Like a genie from a bottle, she was gone in a flash.

Outside, I opened the bag. Chocolate and peanut butter wafted out. How did she know what I was craving? Before I could extract my nose from the bag, I plowed into someone on the sidewalk. "Oh my goodness, I'm so sorry. I... Stan?"

Running into Stan on my way to work was a regular

occurrence. His house lies smack dab in the middle of my trek from Penny Lane to Fulton Street. Running into him, literally, outside a donut shop was a first.

"No worries," he said, picking up sunglasses and a container he dropped when we collided.

"What do you have there, Stan?"

He smiled and held the object up so I could see it was a blue plastic jug. "Found this in the alley behind Dixie's," he said, beaming with pride.

"Ah," I said. Cognizant that any more conversation might drag on longer than necessary, I pretended to be happy for his prized find and hurried away. Working for Jenny was stressful at the best of times, but being late earned me more trouble.

"Yep," he yelled after me. "The garbage trucks won't pick up my bins anymore. Loose needles are a biohazard."

I inhaled deeply and turned around to acknowledge his comment. This might take a while. Perhaps being direct would steer the conversation more quickly toward an end. "Needles?"

I knew about the needles, of course. Whenever I walked by his house on trash pickup day, I saw them lying in his typically open garbage cans. They made him an obvious suspect in Jolee's murder. However, now that I knew Stan better, and the murderer was behind bars, I tried not to think about the needles. Or what might be in the bowling bag Stan usually carried. It was unusual to see him without it, in fact. Or with sunglasses on, which he adjusted over his nose before replying.

"That's right. Needles. See, I have a condition. Psoriatic arthritis. It is painful, let me tell you. Wouldn't wish it on my worst enemy — "

"I am so sorry to hear that." I cut him off because, you

know, Jenny troubles. "Can you tell me more about it another time, Stan? It's just that I am late to work."

His shoulders crumpled. "Oh sure, no problem. Maybe at book club."

His dejected state sent a dagger to my heart. "Or maybe I'll see you on my way from work," I offered, instantly regretting the olive branch. Although harmless, Stan had stalker tendencies that I tried not to encourage.

His eyes lit up. "Yes, I'll look forward to it!" I nodded gratefully and he allowed me to hurry off unimpeded. The blue jug story would at least give us something to talk about when he undoubtedly invited himself to escort me to class.

THREE

Fortunately, walking into the salon ten minutes late went unnoticed by Jenny. Rachel and Linda covered my opening duties. A delivery snafu involving some key hair tinting products kept Jenny attached to the phone in her office while she badgered the vendor all morning. I apologized to Rachel and Linda and made a plan to arrive early tomorrow with their favourite beverages, a mocha for Linda and a chai latte for Rachel.

Since my primary responsibilities depended upon the undelivered tinting products, clients had no use my foiling services. After sweeping the shop multiple times, I decided studying took priority over trivial tasks. Sneaking away, however, was not in the cards for me.

"Hi Daisy." Jenny accosted me as I grabbed my purse.

I jumped, not expecting her in the break room. She wasn't fond of taking breaks. She wasn't fond of anyone else taking breaks.

"Oh Jenny, I didn't expect you. Hi! I was just —"

"Leaving work early." She handed me the purse I came for and tasered me with her eyes. A wide, fake smile stretched around her teeth. "Remind me again why I'm paying you." She shoved a box off the ratty lounge chair and sat.

Oh boy. This would not be a short conversation. "Look, I'm really sorry, Jenny. Other than sweeping, I can't add much value without tinting supplies. Any update on delivery?" I slung my purse over my shoulder to appear nonchalant. The purse slipped down my arm and thudded to the floor.

Jenny never took her eyes off me. "Right, and did my sister allow you to come and go as you please? Because I think checking in with the boss would be a prerequisite." She thumped her hand to her chest, emphasizing her designation as the boss.

She had a valid point. Why was I sneaking off and being late so often? This was never part of my character when Jolee ran the salon. Jolee and I had been like sisters though. We understood each other. Supported each other. We were friends more than co-workers. Jolee did a bossy voice when I wasn't taking care of myself. She hadn't been shy about ordering me around. Jenny was different. She was pure boss without the softness of Jolee's big heart.

"You're right," I told Jenny. "I should have checked in with you before leaving early to study."

Jenny nodded. "Apology accepted. I assume this won't happen again? Arriving late? Sneaking out early?"

"I'll be sure and check with you in both cases." I picked up my purse and wiped a small hair off it. I guess I didn't sweep the break room as well as I could have.

"Yes, you will." Jenny slapped her hands on her thighs while thrusting herself out of the chair. "Your pay will reflect the reduction of hours your absence has cost me. Have a good night."

. . .

ALTHOUGH LIVING with Paula helped me pay for tuition and save up for a car and apartment, I sometimes wondered if going into debt for a place of my own might be worth the peace. One night Paula hosted a cake tasting party as she considered types best suited for book club gatherings. Another night, she brought in local authors to help her evaluate best practices for choosing books. At each of these events, dozens of neighbours and strangers crammed into our home to observe and provide input on various aspects of book club development. Many of these gatherings lasted deep into the night, which was prime studying time for me.

Today Paula had introduced something new to create chaos around my study time. As I stepped through the door, weary from the spanking I had just received from Jenny, an explosion of puppies greeted me. Leaping, drooling, ear-flapping, tail-wagging, high-energy creatures frolicked around my ankles as I tried to keep from tripping down the hallway.

"Don't be mad," Paula said, as a springy beagle repeatedly bounced into my knees. "They aren't staying long." How long they were staying was not the first question on my mind. I had so many questions. "But now that you're home, I need a favour."

Before I could object, let alone change into comfortable clothes, she handed me a thermos and a backpack full of books. "I need you to fill in at the museum. There have been some security breaches and I know you need the money. So I told them you could man the security desk tonight."

"What? For how long?" I tried, but could not keep the whiny tone from my voice. "I have class tonight, Mom."

"Oh poodle nuggets," she exclaimed. "I'll try to find someone to cover you later." Now she was turning me around back toward the front door. "But meanwhile, hurry. They needed someone there hours ago."

As I left, my stomach growled. Darned if I didn't leave those tasty donuts Sadie gave me at the salon. I was looking forward to eating those between work and school.

I filled in for Mom and Rita at the museum often, and even conducted tours when asked. Aside from the inconvenience, the museum paid good money, and there were plenty of lulls between visitors to eke in some studying. Also, the history of the museum fascinated me. Between the resource material offered at the front desk and googling for more tidbits about the resident poet who once lived in there, I felt like I knew James Whitcomb Riley in the flesh.

Scholars praised his idyllic prose, but I glimpsed the poet behind the words. He loved travelling. He worked hard. He was dirt poor. These aspects of his life were well documented. All his roving, publishing and scrabbling for cash came with a price. If you dug deep enough, you could read between the lines. The sad part no one mentioned was that he would never marry the love of his life. Nor would he have children of his own to count among the ones who adored him, listening raptly at his feet to his poetry.

After Paula rushed me out the door, I was not as keen to be at the museum as usual. I was tired. So tired that I fell asleep on top of the law books Paula so thoughtfully packed up for me.

Drifting off at the museum was not unusual. This night was different. I awoke with a sense I was late for class, which I was. I also couldn't shake off the vague memory of Sadie stopping by the museum. Was it a dream? I wasn't sure. Why a Dixie Donut employee would come to the museum after hours, I couldn't say. Even more perplexing was the face that materialized as the haze from my nap dissipated. I was staring into the dead poet's eyes when I woke up. Clearly, this must have been a nightmare or trick of the mind, but I had no time to process the conundrum.

Irritably, I realized Mom hadn't sent anyone to fill in for me. Gathering up my books, I rushed to class and tried my best to press the strange museum encounters to the back of my mind.

FOUR

The next day I woke up with a cat and two beagle puppies sleeping on top of me. That was the first different thing. Also different was the Great Dane licking my face; a feeling akin to driving through a car wash with open windows. By now, I was used to the unpredictability of my mother and the unsustainable living conditions her behaviour created. Sleeping with animals and face licking were not entirely unexpected.

"Paula?" I yelled. "Down, boy," I commanded the giant dog, who obeyed. No reply from Paula, not that she could provide any explanation that would satisfy me. I nudged the puppies off and avoided a claw swipe from the cat.

Somehow I showered, found appropriate attire (black pleather skirt, knee boots and a cotton wrap-around sweater kept in place with a jewelled brooch), and brought Linda's latte and Rachel's tea to the salon on time. Jenny stopped to greet me, assessing my outfit approvingly and raising an eyebrow at the Snickers bar latte I brought for her. The morning was going well. I finished my signature latte from

Petra's and a raspberry beret donut from Dixie between my floor sweeping and hair foiling duties.

When I asked to leave early, Jenny reminded me with stern eyes that she would adjust my pay. So much for hoping the donuts I left in the break room would soften her up.

I picked up an escort from Stan on my way home. He gave more details about needles and waste disposal rules than I cared to know along the way, pausing just long enough for me to grab my law books from home before continuing his explanations all the way to Mass Avenue. "This is where I hop off the escort train. Thanks, Stan," I prompted, to discourage him from following me inside.

These were all fairly normal happenings from my weekly calendar: coffee stop, work, touching base at home, therapy for my trust issues... What would be different about this day: a reality check from my family law professor, a mysterious note in my locker, a last-minute shift at the museum security desk, and a ghost chat.

Before I get into all of that, I should begin with therapy at Grandma's.

"HI GRANDMA." I poked my head into her office. A middle-aged man was crying on her couch.

"Hey there, Dipsy Doodle," she replied. "Can you give us a minute?"

"Oops. Sorry." I closed the door and sat in the waiting area across from the receptionist's desk.

Grandma is a clinical psychologist. Her receptionist since forever, Eileen, is rarely at her desk, which means Grandma's patients are often interrupted. That none of her clients has quit is a testament to Grandma's skill and charm.

I picked up a Psychology All Day magazine and leafed through it, trying to ignore yelps of despair from Grandma's office and a shrivelled up plant by the window with a full watering can beside it.

Eileen burst through the doors. "Aha! I didn't miss you. How the heck are you Daze-a-roo? Aren't you a sight for sore eyes?" She came at me for a hug as her diet cola sloshed over the rim.

"I'm well, Eileen. Great to see you too." I orchestrated a side-hug maneuver to avoid the sticky spray. "Where are your glasses?" I asked, kissing her cheek.

She patted her face and bumbled around her desk, losing most of her drink in the process. "Well, I'll be darned. Where could they be, Daze-a-lee? I'll be right back." She had not returned by the time Grandma came out with her patient, who left the office laughing and smiling.

I walked into her office and made myself comfortable on the yellow velvet couch. "Glen," I heard Grandma say, "I'll send you the bill. Best not to wait for Eileen."

Grandma marched through the office door, turning her attention to me. "What progress have we made this week?" she asked, not wasting any time.

Before I opened my mouth, she closed some imaginary drapes between us before sitting at her desk across from me. She calls this phantom screen our *cone of silence*, a term I now realize law firms use to create an ethical barrier where there might be conflicts of interest. She takes off her grandma hat and puts on her psychologist one.

I smiled. "No hug? No 'how's my favourite grand-daughter?'"

She bristled. "Certainly not. Inappropriate." She suppressed a grin as she smoothed her skirt. "Any progress then?" she repeated, picking up a pen and tapping her desk impatiently.

I sighed. Here we go. "Well, let's see. I had coffee with Brett. He's still just as cute as ever. So far, I haven't screwed that up."

"Why would you screw up with Brett?" A rhetorical question, but I answered it anyway.

"Because of my *daddy approval issues*," I said with air quotes. She nodded, but I knew she wanted to put on her grandma hat and reassure me that Dad loves me and only wants me to be happy. Which would be a conflict of interest because he is her son.

"Moving on then. What else?" she said, her pen tapping.

"Okay, a weird thing happened last night. You're going to think I'm nuts."

She gave me a stern look over her reading glasses. "Disquieting events do not label a person. A person labels a person. Come on then. Out with it."

"Right. Tell me what to label this sequence of events." Aware of time slipping by faster in her office than other places, I plunged ahead. "Paula made me fill in at the museum, which was fine. I can study there."

"Made you fill in. Why?"

"Oh, some security breach, ya-da, ya-da, ya-da, they needed someone, she was busy with the dogs..."

"Dogs?"

"Grandma —"

"Dr. McCartney," she corrected.

"Dr. McCartney. Sorry. The story is not about Mom and the dogs. It's about what happened at the museum."

Grandma gave me the side eye as she smoothed her skirt some more. She was probably counting to ten and picturing that invisible screen between us so she could put her listening hat back on. One exhale later, she was back to her unflappable doctor self. "Of course. Please continue."

"I must have been exhausted, because one minute I was studying and the next I was asleep at the desk."

"Understandable," she said. "Then what?"

"When I woke up, James Whitcomb Riley was standing in the hallway reciting poetry. He looked right at me. I swear it felt real."

"The poet, who died a hundred years ago. Was standing in the hallway?"

"I know. No such thing as ghosts."

"I wouldn't say that."

"But I have been reading about him. It must have been so hard trying and failing to make a living all those years before finally achieving critical acclaim when it was too late to be with the woman he loved, and I guess I... Wait. You wouldn't say what?"

"I would not say 'ghosts do not exist.'" Grandma deadpanned.

I waited for her to explain, but she just sat there, blinking matter-of-factly.

"Are you saying I might have seen a ghost?"

"I'm saying I would not dismiss the possibility that you saw a ghost. I would question it, yes. But not dismiss it. Being open to that which we don't understand or know to be true is a sign of strength."

This was a Grandma I didn't know. I knew the "come over for cookies and cards" Grandma, and the "tell me your darkest secrets, nothing can shock me" Grandma. I hadn't seen this side: the "paranormal science may be legitimate" Grandma. "Okay," I said. "Good to know."

"Then what happened?"

"Well, I realized I was late for class and left. But there is one more thing. When I woke up this morning, I remembered someone visiting me at the museum. Someone in the flesh. Not a ghost."

"Did you know this person?"

"Yes. Well, I met her recently. Her name is Sadie. She works at Dixie Donuts."

"Yummy donuts," Grandma said, her eyes glazing over for a second.

"Right?" I expected my stomach to growl just thinking about donuts. Then I remembered I had breakfast for a change.

"Have you tried the caramelized apple ones?" Grandma wanted to know.

"No, but now I'm craving them."

"The cinnamon frosting alone."

We sat, reflecting on our favourite donuts, before Grandma noticed the clock on the wall behind me and realized we were almost out of time. "So what you are saying is you think Sadie stopped by the museum to see you, even though you barely know her," Grandma prompted. "But you are not sure?"

"Right. Perhaps it was a dream. Like the poet."

Grandma nodded. "Perhaps. I think we must end here, Daisy. Same time next week?"

We had a standing appointment on Wednesdays. "Yes. Thanks for listening."

"It's my job."

"I know. Thanks anyway."

She smiled stiffly before pushing herself to a standing position. I knew not to leave the room until she rolled back the *cone of silence* curtain.

She escorted me to the waiting area where a young

woman staring at her phone gave Grandma a shy smile. Eileen was nowhere in sight.

"Daisy," Grandma said. "I should tell you that hypnosis can be a helpful option for delving more deeply into certain unexplained phenomena."

"Really?" This was another pseudo-science I didn't expect my rather practical grandmother to espouse.

She shrugged. "It's a technique in which I am well trained."

She turned to the girl on the couch, whose phone tapping had stalled when Grandma said the word hypnosis. "Lorna, you may go in now." Then she gave me a big, warm, grandmotherly hug as Lorna sauntered past us. "Bye, darling. See you next week."

"HELLO, RIPLEY," I said to the parrot living downstairs from Grandma's office. He was especially majestic in the sunlight. Red, yellow, and green feathers gleamed as he preened himself by the store window.

"Ripley wants a cracker," the bird said.

I never brought crackers, but we always discussed it. "I do not have a cracker today," I said. "Maybe next time I will bring a donut."

"Ripley wants a donut," he said, which made me laugh. He was a funny one. "Jimmy wants a donut," the parrot said. He was being unusually loquacious.

"Jimmy, huh?" I said. "And who is Jimmy?"

"Jimmy wants a donut," Ripley repeated.

"Daisy, nice to see you!" Mr. Stout, owner of the shoe store, joined Ripley and me by the window.

"Hi Mr. Stout. Ripley wants a donut today," I informed him.

Mr. Stout raised a thick grey eyebrow, and then chuckled. "Who doesn't?" He had a pair of burgundy pumps in his hands, which he placed on the window display platform where an autumn scene was under construction. "Got a minute, Daisy? I have some sparkly shoes to show you." He pointed to an aisle across from the window, where my crow like eyes zoned in on a pair of black flats covered in glitter.

"Oh, wow!" I said, slipping out of my Sketchers. Mr. Stout knows what I like. I admired them for a minute, watching glints of light bounce around the shiny particles before stepping into them. "Mr. Stout, is there a Jimmy that Ripley talks to?"

He brought over a small floor mirror for me. "Hmm, I don't know. Many of my customers talk to Ripley. Some of them try to teach him their names."

"I see. Can I bring him a donut next time? Maybe just a crumb?"

Mr. Stout shook his head. "Sorry, Daisy. Sugar isn't good for parrots. He likes fruit for treats."

I smiled. "I understand. Thanks, Mr. Stout. I have to get going." I removed the shoes and handed them over. These are great. Can I think about it?"

"Of course," he said. "See you next week."

I smiled widely at Ripley as I turned to leave.

"Ripley likes fruit," he said.

"Of course you do," I said.

"Jimmy likes donuts," he added.

FIVE

Talking to Ripley and trying on shoes made me late to class. Again. I stopped at my law school locker and, as I removed the book I needed, a folded up piece of paper fell onto the floor. In class, while Professor Mango droned on about prenuptial agreements, I discretely unfolded the piece of paper. Silently thanking the student in the back row who makes it his mission to keep the professor off topic with pointless questions, I smoothed out the paper on my lap. On it was a handwritten poem.

"To make the world a friendly place,

One must show it a friendly face."

— An Admirer

It was a James Whitcomb Riley quote. One of my favourites. I looked around at my classmates, but no one made eye contact. Some were taking notes. Some were listening to the professor. A few were trying not to laugh at questions from the keener at the back.

After class, Professor Mango stopped me on my way out. I assumed he was going to chastise me for being a bit late to class.

"I am sorry I was late, Professor," I began.

"Miss McCartney," he interrupted. "Are you aware I work at the museum?"

"The museum, sir?" Perhaps there was a family law museum I didn't know about.

"I run creative writing workshops for the students."

Was he talking about the James Whitcomb Riley Museum? I was vaguely aware of field trip programs the museum offered at the reception hall on the property, but I had yet to venture over there. I did not want to offend him, so I chose a neutral response. "No, I didn't know that."

He cleared his throat. "Creative writing is a passion of mine. Teaching law, on the other hand, is a job."

I smiled. A passion shared by one late poet, I thought to myself.

"James Whitcomb Riley," he continued (was he reading my thoughts?), "pursued his passion as a job."

"He did," I answered, not sure where this was going. "Did you know he made money in lots of ways? Selling tonics, and...?"

"Miss McCartney, would you like to know why you are here right now?" Professor Mango interrupted.

"Please," I said, mentally zipping my lips.

"You are currently failing my class."

My heart skipped a beat as my stomach dove through the floor. I mean, I knew not to expect any top of the class awards, but this news shook me. "Failing, sir?"

"You are always late, you are rarely prepared, and your midterm was abysmal."

"I failed the midterm?"

"You barely passed. May I give you some advice?"

"Anything that would help me get up to speed, please. I'm so sorry. I'm sure I am not the only student working full-time, but I have a new boss who is not as accommodating as (I could not utter Jolee's name without exploding into tears)... and I live with my mother who can be (Great, now I was rambling)... erratic, and I fill in at the museum for her from time to time, and I guess the past year has been... a lot..." Stop talking, Daisy, I chided myself. This was not helpful. I swallowed a ball of nerves and clenched my fist around the piece of paper with the poem to keep from crying.

Professor Mango was a statue of apathy. "If you're done?"

"Yes," I whispered.

"Here's my advice. At some point in life, one must choose. It might be an easy choice. It might be a hard one. There may be pros and cons for the various choices. In any event, one still must choose. Like the poet. You must pick a path. And focus."

"Do you mean law versus hair styling, sir?"

"I'm not interested in the specific choices plaguing you at the moment, Miss McCartney. However, I will say this. You are doing a disservice to the study of law. The law profession is a valiant one. From where I stand, you are not worthy of it."

This was not new information, I thought, as I left the classroom. Yes, I had too many irons in the fire. Petra was just telling me the same thing, wasn't she? She said I would figure it out. Grandma thinks I'll figure it out.

Actually failing family law though? That was news, the irony of which was not lost on me. I was not over Farley giving up on me. I was not over Dad walking away from Mom. In place of a fractured family, I scrambled to cobble together a replacement. But then Jolee died. One more departure to not get over. Of course, I was failing at family law. Nothing about families was intuitive for me. What did I really know about families?

As I stood staring blankly into my locker moments later, I realized that maybe failing at family law was part of figuring it out.

I opened the note, still crunched in my fist, and read it again. Could the note be from Professor Mango? He would certainly be familiar with Riley's poetry, given our conversation. I glanced left down the hallway, then right, like the note's author would suddenly appear from around a corner. "Okay, Daisy, shake it off," I mumbled, before throwing the note in the trash. Then I noticed a text from Mom.

"Can you fill in at the museum again? Thanks honey."

Like the rudderless law student hair stylist museum security person I was, I grabbed one more book from my locker and set out for Lockerbie Street. If I was to spend the night at a security desk, I might as well fill my head with family law cases.

SIX

Once behind the desk, I wasted no time turning the pages of my textbook to prenuptial agreements. My plan was simple: master tonight's topic and then work backwards to study what I had missed. Before long, I realized prenups are just a melding of property and contract law principles — principles I learned first year of law school. As I worked my way through the family law subtopics, I took careful notes on the various judicial decrees over domestic abuse, spousal arrangements, and unconscionable clauses.

My phone buzzed with a text from Brett.

Are you at home?

Hi-ya handsome. No, I am at the museum. Wanna meet up later? ;)

:) Unfortunately, I am working. Text me when you leave and when you get home.

Why the sudden concern? Is there an axe murderer on the loose?

Maybe. Seriously, though.

Okay. I'll text you, oh knight in shining armour.

I wondered why Brett's hackles were up. True, he was a thoughtful person. Also true, I was almost murdered once after he tried to warn me. After I recovered, and justice was served, he hadn't been paranoid about my safety. Whatever his concern, I looked forward to drilling him about it later.

Perhaps his paranoia had me on edge, but as I sat staring at Brett's text, I heard a noise. It sounded like a skittering of something across the stone flooring; vaguely mouse-like. Not that rodents freak me out. Mice have their agendas and I have mine. Wasting nervous energy on tiny nocturnal creatures was not a chief concern.

My stomach made a low growl that echoed through the cavernous hallway. At least I hoped it was my stomach. When had I last eaten? Right, that morning. It was now past dinnertime, and one latte and a donut do not a meal plan make. The second growl was definitely in my stomach, and now I was thinking about raspberry donuts.

Do you smell them as well?

I looked around. Did someone just say something? This is what happens when I go too long without food, stomach growling, followed by my brain going all weird.

There was a man here eating what you call a donut. They came and took him away, but I can still smell it.

"Hello?" I called to the empty hallway. "Is there someone here?"

I opened the drawer and grabbed a flashlight. I suppose I could have turned on some proper lighting, but at that point, I honestly believed my nutrient starved brain was the culprit. Still, when one hears voices, one should investigate. Particularly if one is in charge of security for a place. Even if one hallucinates when hungry.

I walked into the parlour, aiming my light into every nook, chesterfield, and cranny. Nothing. Then I lit up the bookshelves in the library. Nothing there either. I inspected the kitchen and bathrooms. Nothing. Not even a mouse. While upstairs, I investigated the master bedroom and hallways. Look at me, acting like a proper security guard, I thought, rather than sitting at a table studying all night.

I paused outside Riley's room. This was the place where he spent most of his time at the end of his life. I stepped over the velvet rope and wandered around. No one ever sat in the wicker chair. It was old and fragile, not to mention the poet's favourite sitting spot. I glanced at the bed, his final resting place, with a shiver. According to the tour notes, he was sleeping when the second stroke got him. Remembering that tidbit, I sat down and uttered a quiet prayer.

"I hope you are at peace now, Mr. Riley," I whispered.

You realize you are in my chair.

Ha! Exactly what I thought he would say. If he were here now, I wonder if we would have a witty conversation. "Is it your chair?" I pretend parried. "I don't see your name on it."

Got me there. Anyway, you must be tired. Better you rest there than at the security desk.

I wonder if security desks existed in his time. I allowed myself to lean back and rock a little for a moment. "Sorry," I said, gripping the arms to stand up. "I am being disrespectful." No one aside from cleaning staff was allowed behind the velvet rope, let alone in the wicker chair.

I accept your apology, but do not get up. It has been too long since I have conversed. Please continue. I shall sit at the edge of my bed.

"Mr. Riley, you are a true gentleman," I said. Then, unless my fuel-deprived brain was playing tricks on me again, I saw the mattress sag a fraction, as if under the

sudden weight of a person. I convinced myself I had imagined it, blaming low blood sugar and loneliness for my over-
active inner thoughts. The words, his and mine, felt like a
conversation taking place entirely in my head. Here I was in
the great poet's room. Where better to get lost in a pretend
conversation with James Whitcomb Riley?

*If I were a true gentleman, I would not be entertaining
an unescorted young lady in my bedroom.*

I laughed, because that was probably true. "I trust you
will keep your hands to yourself then," I joked.

His turn to laugh. *You have my word.*

I sat back in the wicker chair and let the magnificence of
his authentically appointed room soak in. It gave me a new
appreciation for the little stick house Paula and I renovated.
What a wonderful time it must have been, being around
when the Victrola was invented (I gazed at the one in
Riley's room, which was probably not the original one he
enjoyed) and being served grand dinners in the elegant
dining room. Sad too, I realized, for those who could not
afford pleasures such as this. "I certainly could not afford to
live this way," I realized.

*Have you not found a gentleman to care for you and
support you?*

"Well, Mr. Riley. Today, women pursue their own
means of support." I thought of Clara when she and the
poet met. She was a schoolteacher, boarding in the Riley's
house. "And not just teaching or nursing," I added. "I am
studying to be a lawyer, plus developing skills for styling
hair. It is good to have choices, but I have to say, Mr. Riley,
women of your time would turn over in their graves to know
what a travesty I am making of my choices."

The practice of law is a fine profession.

I nodded. "Yes, it is." No comment on hair styling, I

noted. Women wore their hair long in Riley's time. Perhaps there was no such thing as a hair stylist then. "My father would agree with you. I suppose I am living in the past. When my friend was alive, being a part of her hair salon was like being in a family where expectations were few and laughter was plentiful."

Perhaps we are both living in a place we no longer belong.

My eyes, which had grown heavy, sprung open. I stood up and crossed the floor to the bed, still with an imaginary rump sized dent. Suppose he was actually here, and I was really having a conversation with James Whitcomb Riley! I thought about Grandma, whose brilliant mind remained open to the possibility of ghosts. What had she said? She would question it, yes, but not dismiss it?

I walked away from the bed and gazed out the window, wondering what question I could ask. If Riley truly were here in this room, what would I want to know? I supposed 'why was he talking to me' would be first on the list. Of all people, why me?

My phone's alarm blared, jolting me from my musings. My shift was over. Time to go home.

"Thank you for the conversation, Mr. Riley. I hope we can do this another time," I said, ambling toward the front door.

"Leaving now," I texted Brett.

Great. Let me know when you're home safely.

It was not until I locked the door and turned to leave that the reply I surely imagined came.

I have nothing but time.

SEVEN

When I got home, I texted Brett from the front porch.

HOME SAFE AND SOUND. Mind telling me why the sudden interest in my comings and goings?

Thank you. Someone died in the museum last night. I didn't want to freak you out with that information while you were there.

Now I'm freaking out. Who? Someone I know? What happened?

No one you know and it's not public knowledge yet. He took a tumble down the stairs. Probably an accident.

That's terrible. It must have happened after...

I BACK-SPACED over the last five words and sent only the two-word sentence.

It must have happened after I left last night. Could

Sadie, who may or may not have come to visit, have had something to do with it? Now I was not sure what to think about seeing Riley in the hallway. What if it wasn't Riley? What if it was someone dressed like him? Someone who fell down the stairs or pushed someone else? But why would someone dress in period garb from the last century? I should tell Brett what I knew, right? Whether Sadie's or Riley's presence actually happened, withholding information relevant to a police case would be unethical. My tenuous observations might be useful information for the investigation.

Still, what stopped me from telling Brett about my shift at the museum last night? With mounting alarm, I realized the reason I held back. What if the man's fall was not accidental? What if he was murdered? I would become a suspect in the murder.

I dashed up the stairs to my room. Where were all the pets? The house was eerily quiet. I clicked on my desk light and paced the room, suddenly wide awake, my heart thumping hard against my ribs cage. I breathed in and out the way I do before making a presentation in class; slow measured breaths to calm myself. Once my heartbeat was subdued, I tried to think rationally.

Who knew I was working there last night? Grandma knew, but anything I told her in therapy fell under doctor patient privilege. On the other hand, was I confusing lawyer client privilege with psychology? She would never discuss what her patients say at therapy. I knew that much. Were there exceptions? *Except with murder,* types of exceptions? Suddenly I felt lightheaded. My sight blurred. I sat down on the bed with my head between my knees, trying not to obsess. Trying not to focus on what I knew about lawyers. Lawyers cannot reveal client conversations. Unless the information is necessary to protect public safety. If Sadie or a man in costume or a dead poet were walking around in the museum on the night someone died, if they had a part in someone's death, they could hurt someone again.

I needed to think like a lawyer. I needed to balance the various options and weigh their potential impact. Before giving Brett potentially useless information, a clear head was required. I should eat, sleep, and ensure my brain was working on full tilt. As far as I knew, the only people who knew I worked at the museum last night were Paula and Grandma. And possibly Sadie. If Sadie really was at the museum, what if she, I don't know, drugged me and pushed someone down the stairs? Still, it may have been an accident; probably was an accident, Brett said. The best course was to do nothing until I had more information. Otherwise, I could become murder suspect number one.

It was past midnight now. Paula would be sound asleep. Thank goodness there were no yapping dogs or skulking cats to announce my presence. Not a creature stirred. Not even a mouse.

Stepping quietly down the stairs to the kitchen, I giggled at my little joke. Mice I could handle. That Great Dane would be a shock to meet in a dark house.

I opened the refrigerator, elated to find leftover pesto lasagna inside. As I waited for the microwave to do its thing, my mind wandered from mice to Great Danes and back to mice again. There were mice in the museum tonight, I remembered. Or I thought there were mice. But I did not find any. I had a nice pretend conversation with Mr. Riley instead.

Unless it wasn't a pretend conversation. Unless I was speaking with a ghost. A ghost who knew I was there at the museum. That is when I remembered what was nagging at my addled brain. What had he said? Just before I searched the house looking for a mysterious voice?

No matter how hard I tried, I could not remember. Something about smelling a donut. And a man, I thought? If the ghost of James Whitcomb Riley was actually speaking to me tonight, he may have seen what happened the night before. Which means I needed to grab another security desk shift as soon as possible. Before I became a murder suspect.

EIGHT

"Mom, does the museum need a security person today?"

"Good morning to you, too."

I kissed her cheek. "Sorry. How are you this morning?"

Paula was cleaning out the refrigerator. She handed me a moldy chunk of cheese. "Good! Put this in the compost, please?"

I did as I was told. "You're not throwing out the lasagna, are you?"

She handed me a container with an inch of ice cream at the bottom and at least four inches of ice on top. "Of course not. Do something with that, will you?"

"Sure." I looked around, trying to decide where best to let a container of ice cream melt. A dumpster? I popped it in the microwave. Then zeroed in on the coffee pot. "Yes, coffee! Thanks for making it."

Paula stood up and brushed off her knees. "I think that's got it. Been awhile since I cleaned out the fridge."

The microwave dinged. I rinsed a glop of goo into the sink and disposed of the container. Then I leaned against the counter, cradling my coffee cup. "I can't help but notice," I said, widening my arms, "the pitter patter of no little feet in the house."

She smirked. "Not today," she said. "Yet."

"Are you running a pet daycare or a kennel? Do we need money?" This was the only explanation I could think of for the variety of specimens running through the house lately.

"Help me pull the fridge away from the wall a bit," she said.

Together we wiggled the awkward appliance, corner by corner until a six-inch area between its back and the wall presented itself. I handed her the broom.

"Not a daycare or kennel," she said as she swept up enough dog hair to knit a sweater.

I brought her the trash can, and she dumped the mound of fluff with the help of a dustbin.

"Well. I was thinking about what Stan said," Mom continued.

"Really? About what?"

"You know, about making the book club about a purpose. Other than reading."

I took a sip of coffee. Mom actually listened to Stan. I couldn't help grinning as I mentally pressed a gold star to her forehead.

"I looked into pet rescue organizations, and I found one quite close to Lockerbie."

"Is this where you beg me for a dog and I ask you who is going to feed it and water it and take it for walks?" I joked.

"Har-dee-har-har. No, but what I learned is that the rescue facilities are often overwhelmed with strays. They don't like to turn down any animal, so they need foster volunteers as much as they need adoptive families."

"Hmm, I guess that makes sense. I suppose the rescues

put potential owners thorough a vetting process while the adopted pets wait for homes."

"Exactly. In cramped conditions, often," Paula added.

"So I can expect random pets here on a regular basis?"

"I'm afraid so."

I shrugged. "I could get used to that."

"Who knows?" Paula said, shoving the fridge against the wall with her backside. "Maybe I will adopt one someday." She found her coffee cup in the sink and filled it up again. "More?"

I tilted my still full cup at her. "I'm good, thanks."

"So. What were you nattering about when you first flew in here?"

"Oh, I wanted to ask about taking more museum shifts. I don't mind staffing the security desk. It's peaceful there. I can study."

She eyed me skeptically. "You can study anywhere."

"True, but not while making money."

"I'll find out if they need someone tonight," Paula said. "Oh, and your grandmother called. The one that doesn't like me."

I huffed. "Grandma doesn't not like you. Is she cancelling therapy next week?"

"I don't know. I didn't take a message. Seemed the opposite. Another opening, maybe?"

"That's odd. I'll call her later. I want to swing by Petra's before heading to the salon. You'll text if they need me at the museum?"

Mom nodded. "Rita and I are doing some tours there this afternoon. I'll let you know. Oh, and some mail came for you. I put it on the coffee table in the parlour. What was the letter Martin handed you the other day?"

She saw that? Should I tell her? A part of me didn't

want to dredge up news about my ex sooner than I had to. But lying to Mom wasn't something I felt comfortable doing. Then I remembered Petra taking the letter from me. "Something for Petra," I mumbled, averting my eyes.

Mom wasn't buying it. I could see feel her head tilting at me, and busied myself wiping down the counter by the coffeepot. "I saw Martin hand it to *you*," she said.

"I was standing right next to Petra." I said, lamely.

Thankfully, the doorbell spared me from of the third degree. "I'll get that on my way out."

"BRETT?" I opened the door to a very handsome man in uniform; one who did not look especially happy to see me. "Is everything okay?" I hoped this would not be that moment where I would be handcuffed and advised of my rights. "I know my rights." Oh dear. I said that out loud.

"What rights?" He cocked his head and narrowed his eyes.

I decided to just go with it. "If you are here to arrest me, I know my rights. You have to have cause, you have to..."

He burst out laughing. Thank goodness. "Why would I be here to arrest you?"

I shrugged. There was no acceptable answer. So instead of answering him, I asked another question. "Why are you here, then?"

He leaned against the doorframe, milking my awkwardness for all it's worth. "To walk with you for coffee? Say hello? Make sure you're okay?"

What a relief. His visit wasn't about a potential murderer on the loose. He was being protective. He didn't know I was suspect number one yet. Gosh, I really hope I didn't say any of those things out loud.

"This is where you say something like, 'I'd love to join you for coffee,' or 'Hello back,' or 'What else can we do with those handcuffs?'"

Now I was laughing. And turning red. Bright cherry red, judging by the raging fire in my cheeks. I playfully smacked his arm, where a very firm bicep did not budge. Oh great, now the heat was spreading to my neck. "Stop it." I whispered, checking behind me and noting with relief that Paula was out of earshot. "Paula's here."

"Good. I wanted to see her too, actually."

My ears twitched. "Really? Why?"

"Nothing you need to worry about."

If he was going to ask her who was at the museum the other night, I was not ready for that. "Can you talk to her later? You promised me coffee."

"Like the kind in your hand?"

Well, would you look at that? I was still holding my coffee cup. Luckily, it wasn't empty. "Absolutely not. I want some real coffee."

"Okay," he laughed. "Let's go."

He left the squad car parked in front of the house. He would be back, I realized, with pesky questions for Paula. Maybe I could find out more at breakfast.

After buying lattes from Petra, I wanted to swing by Dixie Donuts. Not for donuts this time. Okay, maybe for donuts. But also to quiz Sadie about her museum appearance. I hoped I could broach the subject without Brett overhearing. Could be tricky.

"So," I said as we headed down Lockerbie Street. "Is there any more information on the man that fell down the stairs?" I crossed my fingers, hoping his demise was indeed an accident. Or that they had a suspect other than me.

"Not really. The operating theory is still accidental death. He had been eating a donut, apparently."

"Ew. How do you know that?"

"Ew? We didn't pump his stomach, Daisy. There were crumbs on his face. And half a donut at the bottom of the stairs."

"I guess I pictured some pathologist cutting open his stomach."

"That will only happen if there is something suspicious in the donut. We sent it off for testing."

I stopped walking. We were right in front of the Riley museum. A sudden gust of wind sent a shiver up my spine. "Do you think someone poisoned him?"

Brett shrugged. "We have to be thorough."

Together, we turned toward the mansion. Without leaves, the trees stood like skeletal guards on the lawn. I could not help thinking the place had taken on a haunted quality. I wondered how many people died in that house over the last century.

"I feel bad for his fiancée," Brett said, jolting my attention back to him.

"He was engaged? How sad. How did you know that?" I mean, it's not as if men typically wear engagement rings.

Brett took my hand and pulled me back to walking. "It was in the records at the visitor's center. He and his fiancée were going to move here from Bloomington and marry at the museum next summer."

"Hmm, small world." I mused, as we turned off Lockerbie onto East. A line from one of Riley's poems suddenly popped into my head.

. . .

FOR NO LANGUAGE *could frame and no lips could repeat*
My rhyme-haunted raptures of Lockerbie Street

"WHAT DO YOU MEAN?" Brett asked.

"What?" Had I said the poem aloud?

"I said they were moving here from Bloomington and you said 'small world?'"

"Oh, right. Sorry, I was just remembering a great line from one of Riley's poems."

I wondered what Riley meant by rhyme-haunted raptures. "I said 'small world' because Sadie moved here from Bloomington. She mentioned it after you left the donut shop the other day. Dixie Corp. promoted her to manager at the Lockerbie store."

We walked a little further in silence. "I guess I hadn't put that together," Brett said.

"Put what together?"

He put his arm around me. "Never mind, you. If I tell you any more confidential information, I might have to kill you."

NINE

We were halfway to Petra's and Brett had to turn back. The precinct needed him, so he made a dash for his car. (I may or may not have stared at his backside after he kissed me and sprinted away.) I felt badly for his caffeine needs but also felt a bit of relief, knowing he'd pepper Paula with questions another time (or not at all).

I wondered what Brett could tell me about connecting the dots between Sadie being from Bloomington and the man who fell, who was also from Bloomington. Not only did I wonder about it, I was getting a bad feeling about it. I hoped that visit I thought I had from Sadie was part of my sleep-induced hysteria the night I fell asleep at the museum. If it wasn't, the coincidence of the dead man and Sadie being at the same place that evening baffled me. If I was thinking about those dots connecting, I could only imagine what Brett's investigative mind would piece together if he discovered I had also been at the scene of a possible murder. Actually, at the scene before the scene, but still.

Before I could track down Sadie at Dixie Donuts, I wanted to check on Petra. I worried about her business suffering because of Dixie Donuts. Her friendship meant a lot to me. Even as she struggled to keep her business afloat, she took time out of scone making to counsel me on what to do with Farley's letter. I needed to step up and offer her whatever help I could. Perhaps I could give her hair some highlights. Or help her make scones. Or talk philosophy with her.

Whatever I expected when I stopped at Petra's for a latte, it certainly wasn't the scene that unfolded as I rounded the corner of East & Michigan. At first, I thought I was seeing an exceptionally long line from Dixie Donuts, which would be no great surprise. As I drew closer, I realized the line was not coming from Dixie. It started on the other side of Dixie, and it stretched past Cleveland Avenue.

"Excuse me," I asked a woman with a stroller at the end of the line. "Are you waiting for donuts?"

"Donuts?" she laughed. "No, I'm waiting for pie."

Pie? Filled with dread, I stepped up my pace. What if Petra had another competitor? A donut shop on one side and a pie place on the other? That would be tragic. When I finally reached the door of Petra's Pastries, I found a sheet of paper taped over the logo on her store window. On it, in magic marker, was written: "Pie Latte." What the...?

No way was I waiting in that line or fighting my way through the people at the front who likely had been waiting for ages. I dialled Petra on my phone instead.

"Pie Latte," she answered.

"What happened to Petra's Pastries?" I shouted through the phone. I could barely hear her.

"I rebranded. It's loud here in the kitchen. Can I call you back? I'm a little busy at the moment."

But I really wanted a latte. "I was just stopping by to see

if I could help," I lied. I mean, I wanted to help. I also wanted a latte.

"You want a latte, don't you?"

"No. Yes. But I also want to help."

There was a pause. "We only have pie lattes now."

"What the heck is a..."

"Look, if you really want to help, I can let you in the back door and give you an apron. But I don't have time to chitchat."

Oh. "I really want to help."

"Then. Come. To. The. Back," she said in sarcastic staccato.

I hung up, laughing. It was good to hear Petra being sassy. She was having fun, I could tell, and I couldn't wait to hear all about it. As I turned on Cleveland and found the alley behind Petra's store, I called the salon. I was going to be late. Probably very late.

"Hi Jenny," I said, when she answered. "Something has come up. I can't come in today."

"This isn't a freaking company, Daisy," she said. "You don't get personal days and holidays. Are you sick?"

"Do we get sick days?"

"No."

That's too bad. "I'm not sick. I need to help a friend." It felt good to say that. I felt a dopamine hit just uttering the words. I should say them more often.

"Well, I hope your friend is paying you because I'm not."

"I understand. My pay check will reflect the day off. That's fine." I hoped it would be fine. I would need to stop buying lattes for a while, that's for sure.

"No, Daisy. I'm not paying you anything. Ever. You're a lousy employee and you're fired."

Hmm. I did not see that coming. But I was at Petra's back door, with no time to dwell on personal ramifications, so I hung up and decided I would pull a Scarlet O'Hara and worry about that tomorrow.

THE MORNING FLEW by in such a haze; I forgot I was running on black coffee alone. Petra had called in every one of her students who were able and willing to work. Inside the back door, I saw a pie dough mixing station, a kneading and rolling station and another area for forming piecrust into deep-dish versions, lattice versions, and cutesy cutouts. The stove, limited counter space and ovens were crammed with bubbling pie innards in various stages of baking and towers of pie boxes.

Petra started me on pie box folding, and then asked a student to teach me how to make meringue. After that, I graduated to the chocolate pie station from which they had to drag me kicking and screaming. Petra's secret was to add a splash of peanut butter whiskey as the chocolate simmered (don't worry, the alcohol cooks off, she told me, when she saw me eyeing the toddlers in strollers).

By 2:00, we were low on lard and flour, forcing Petra to turn people away. By 3:00, we were sold out. Petra wrote, "Closed" on a box top with a magic marker and taped it to the front door. I was vibrating. The whole experience was so much fun.

While the student workers finished sweeping and wiping down surfaces, Petra made me a pie-flavoured latte. I opted for the peanut butter chocolate pie latte, into which she poured extra whiskey.

"How did this all happen?" I asked, marvelling at the surrounding scene. Petra had dismantled all the pastry cases in the shop. In their place stood a giant workstation with a tiny counter for the cash machine.

"I was honestly so tired of making scones, Daisy," Petra said with a heavy sigh. "All I've done for the last ten years is teach philosophy and make scones. I thought about adding donuts. Anyone can make donuts. But who can compete with Dixie's reputation? I heard someone order a chai latte while I was cutting out pumpkin-shaped scones, and in my head, I heard Pie Latte. I thought, that's it! I could make lattes out of pie flavours. I considered pairing pie lattes with scones, but that is just a horse of a different colour from what I was already doing. So then, it hit me. I could make pies to match the lattes. No one is doing that."

"You must have acted fast. Did you turn this place around overnight?"

"I had help from the students. They were excited about pie. Pie supplies are not much different from scone ingredients; which are mostly various flour types, plus fat to hold it together. We started experimenting with a few basic fillings, but it didn't take long to come up with the winners. People were buying the pies before we had the sign up. The aroma brought them in from outside out of curiosity. Then the word spread and people started asking. Can you make strawberry rhubarb? Key lime?" Petra laughed. "I had one student on standby at Meyers, hunting down ingredients and carting it all downtown."

Petra looked around the shop, beaming with pride. "I have a delivery of flour coming tonight. Some lard in the morning. We will just keep making pies until we figure out how to keep making pies."

I sipped my drink and shook my head. "I could not be more proud of you, Petra. You ran into an obstacle with your business and you pivoted. You made lemonade out of lemons." I wondered if she was thinking about lemonade pie, because now that's what I was thinking. "Thanks for letting me help today. It was fun. I missed you."

"Didn't I just see you a couple of days ago?"

I laughed. "I guess it's been a long couple of days."

"Same," she said.

It was almost 4:00, and I had a class. While Petra locked up, I checked messages and saw one from Paula. It was good news. "Yes! I am filling in at the museum tonight."

Petra looked at me as if my face was a puzzle she couldn't quite solve. "What's going on at the museum, Daisy?"

We were each headed in opposite directions, so I filled her in as quickly as I could. I mentioned the possible Sadie appearance and swore her to secrecy about the man who fell down the stairs. I left out the talking to ghosts part. It was a crucial part of the story, but I still wasn't sure it was real. I told her enough to make her worry about me being a suspect in a potential murder investigation.

"You know that Stalker Stan has been following you, right?"

"Following me? I know if he sees me walk by his house, I get an automatic escort to wherever I'm going. He's harmless, though. I think."

"I hate to tell you this, but I have seen him lurking around the museum in the evenings. Have you ever noticed anyone follow you home?"

My skin felt all creepy crawly. "Follow me home?"

"Just keep an eye out," Petra said, patting me on the shoulder. "Like you said, he's probably harmless."

I nodded. "Okay. Thanks. I'll see you tomorrow."

"What's tomorrow?"

"Pie baking, of course!" Petra smiled back at me as we

parted on the sidewalk. It was the widest smile I had seen on her face in a long while.

I had one more thing to do before heading to class. Talk to Sadie. With my stomach full of chocolate pie latte, I popped into Dixie Donuts to search for the woman with a wonky blond hairdo.

I spotted Sadie behind the counter where she was unpacking paper coffee cups. She wore a skintight black dress with an apron the same colour accented with pink iced donuts. The ensemble gave me a nostalgic pang, realizing half my wardrobe was fancy black salon-appropriate clothing. But I pushed that thought into the back of my mind.

She smiled when I caught her eye. "Daisy, how nice to see you. Did you come for the donut of the day? It's peanut butter cup with maple cream."

Okay, yum. But my tummy was full of a similarly flavoured latte. "Wow that sounds great. How about one to go? I'm still full from, um, breakfast."

"Coming right up." Her smile did not quite reach her eyes, I noticed. Speaking of eyes, one was blue and the other green; something I had not noticed before. I was still staring at them when she handed me the takeout bag. Her hair, slicked back into a tight bun at the nap of her neck, somehow showcased her eyes, which were heavily framed by mascara.

She raised her chin as she caught me gawking. "Sorry. I didn't notice your eyes before." I said. Just as my eyes floated between her two hair nobs before, they were ping ponging again between her eyes. "Do you wear contacts?"

"I have perfect vision," she answered. "What else can I do for you, Daisy?"

That was an odd answer, but then again, how should

one react to gawking? I forced my eyes to the donut menu above her head. "I think I'm good, thank you. I just have a question."

"Yes?"

I sensed customers lining up behind me. Better make this quick. "Did you stop by the museum when I was working the other night?" She would definitely think I was a weirdo, I feared. There was no reason for her to come to the museum so late at...

"I did." She leaned an ear toward one shoulder, forcing me to lock onto her eyes again. "You don't remember?"

Ping. Pong. Ping. Pong... Argh, I needed to move on. "Of course. I was just so tired. I forget things that happen when I'm tired."

"Alice," Sadie said to the server working the dining area. "Could you help these customers at the counter? I'll just be a sec." She and Alice traded places so Sadie could walk me to the door. "Well, you remember I was asking you about the museum's wedding venue services," she said with disconcerting calmness.

Nope. I did not remember that. "Right," I said. This was her reason for coming to the museum at night? To ask about programming services? Why would I have no memory of that conversation? "It's not really my area," I said, hoping I was repeating what I might have told her then. "But if there are any, um, other questions, I can track down the answers for you."

She touched the inside of my elbow, a friendly tap, and there I was again, back to staring into her alluring eyes. "Sadly, there won't be a wedding now."

Wedding. What wedding? "Oh?" I said.

I watched a single tear form in the corner of her green

eye and begin a slow trek along the inside of her nose. "My fiancé passed away two nights ago," she said.

"Oh my goodness, Sadie." Shocked, I immediately hugged her. "I am so sorry."

She delicately disentangled herself from my arms, wiping the tear away. Her eyes darted to some customers who had noticed our exchange. This was her place of business. She did not want to create a scene.

Poor girl needed a friend though. "I should let you get back to work. Is there anything I can do? I know you are new here. Do you have friends in town? Family?"

She sniffed and wiped a sleeve under her eye. "I will be fine, don't worry. Farley and I have supports nearby." Her eyes shot to the bag in my hands. "I should get back. Thanks for the kind words, Daisy."

I nodded and tore my eyes away from hers, barely cognizant of the conversation that had just happened. It wasn't until I was outside on the sidewalk that I realized she had said the name Farley.

TEN

After the opposite of a pep talk I received from Professor Mango this week, I was especially dreading today's course in Administrative Law. Once again, I was under-prepared. Tax, securities, franchise, and environmental rule-making systems buzzed around like bees in my head, with no coherent significance.

But something else was preventing my ability to focus. When Sadie said "Farley and I have supports," did she mean Farley was her fiancé and now he was dead? I wanted to find another explanation, but the dots connected too perfectly: the letter from Farley warning me about possibly seeing him in town and that he had moved on; Sadie recently moving from Bloomington where his family business was headquartered; and the tidbits Brett revealed about his case, particularly a dead man from Bloomington, whose upcoming wedding was registered in the museum's books. If the Farley I once called my boyfriend died, what was he doing at the museum alone at night? Why was Sadie at the museum the same night Farley died?

I was itching for class to be over so I could start my shift at the museum. Even if the ghost wasn't real, I needed time alone to work out what might have happened. The longer I held back information from Brett about my whereabouts the night of the death, the more I dreaded the conversation. He didn't know I was working there. He didn't know about the letter from Farley. Both facts pointed a giant finger in my direction.

"HI, DAISY." I had just flung open my locker door, snagging the law book I needed for class, when a vaguely familiar voice greeted me. Tad was standing on the other side of my locker. Or Ted. Something with a T.

"Hi-ya, fellow legal beagle," I replied, sidestepping the name quandary. He was definitely someone from my Admin class. The one who always had the right answer when the professor called on him. I admired his unflappable spirit and may have stared too long once or twice at his carefully gelled hair. This was the first time he ever acknowledged me.

He thrust out his hand. "It's Tad. Nice to meet you."

We were both late, I realized, as we shook hands and migrated toward class.

"Right, Tad. You are the cool under pressure guy. Can you teach me how to do that?"

He laughed. "I think you hold your own. I've never seen you sweat."

We were almost at the classroom doors when a very rigid, very familiar figure stepped in my way. My father.

Reading the room, Tad veered and kept moving. "See you later," he said.

I stopped short. "Hi Dad." I bent my head toward the doors Tad just disappeared behind. "I'm late to —"

"I know," he said. "This is more important." He took the book out of my hand and led me to the student lounge, where we sat on two high-backed chairs facing each other. "What are you doing?" His face was a mask of disappointment and bafflement I knew all too well. The face he made when I dropped physics for a Family Enterprise course in college. The expression he gave in every instance where I chose a wonky path.

I assumed he was not looking for an answer like "trying to get to class," and he had that scary *you are about to get a lecture* look about him, so I shrugged and waited.

After an exasperated sigh, he leaned back and gripped his chair with white knuckles. "Arnold Mango and I are old friends," he began.

So my Family Law professor had ratted me out, I thought, which was not great news for me. Also, I did not know his first name was Arnold.

"We were law school peers and we serve on a charity board together," he added.

"He told you I am failing his class," I guessed, laying all my cards on the table.

"He told me what I already expected. That your heart is not in this."

I stared down at my law book on his lap. He was right. Did I see myself finessing a bureaucracy of regulators for a company who was delinquent in its taxes, or facing fines for securities violations, or needing construction permits held up by rare nesting turtles? No, I did not. When I thought of practicing law, all I could see were a stack of books filled with cases to analyze. "I wish I knew where my heart wanted to be," I said. "Did you always know you wanted to be a lawyer?"

"Yes," he said, in a matter of fact manner.

My eyes met his and found no wrath in them. Curiously, they had softened into something like concern. "Lucky you," I said.

He nodded, then wagged his head back and forth. "It was an easy choice for me, yes. But I made my share of mistakes. I let my zeal for practicing law overshadow your mother's priorities, for example."

"You hated those renovations."

"I didn't hate the renovations. I hated the chaos they created at home. Spending all day putting my clients' affairs in order filled my cup. Coming home to chaos drained me." He leaned over and patted my knee. "I'm sorry things didn't work out for me and your mom."

He had never said that before. Never had he even acknowledged that moving out was moving out for good, that leaving our house meant seeing me less often, that divorcing mom meant I had two separate parents instead of one unit.

Something locked into place when he said, *I'm sorry.* I realized he never meant to hurt me or Paula. He just didn't want to walk around with an empty cup. "Thanks, Dad. I'm sorry I suck so much at law. I know I'm a big disappointment for you."

He scooted to the edge of his chair and set the book on the floor. His strong hands gripped my arms. "Listen to me," he said, boring his steely blue eyes into mine. "You are not a disappointment. I should have never pushed you to do something I wanted more than you did. I didn't know, until Arnold explained it to me, that you can have more than one passion in life. Law isn't a clear path for everyone like it was for me. You are a bright, curious, fascinating woman, Daisy. It has been a pleasure watching you investigate the world around you, trying out new skills, staying open to new experiences. You are the type of person who will find your cup before it finds you."

I huffed out a sarcastic laugh. "I'm not sure what that means, but thank you." I stared over his shoulder at the doors to the class. "I suppose I should head into class now."

We both stood up and hugged.

"Or not." He grinned and handed me the book. "You do you."

I watched him walk down the hall and stop to slap the back of a man in a suit, exchange a few words, and carry on toward the building's exit. Which is exactly where I headed next.

ELEVEN

As I left my book, locker, and the law school building behind, I noticed a text from Grandma.

I have an opening in my schedule now. Shall we discuss hypnotism?

I wasn't due at the museum for a while, so I replied yes and headed toward Mass Avenue.

Before I got there, I needed to come clean with Brett. He should know I was at the museum that night. He should not have to hear it from someone else. He needed to know about my ex-boyfriend. Also, I needed to know if Farley was the man who died in the museum that night.

My call rolled to voicemail, so I sent him a text:

DO YOU HAVE A MINUTE?

Sorry Daisy, I'm tied up.

Tomorrow then?

Let me call you when I have a minute. My ex just dropped into town out of the blue.

. . .

STUNNED, I reread the last sentence repeatedly until the realization sunk in: I wasn't the only one in the dark about an ex. I knew he had an ex, but he never talked about her. Not only did we avoid discussing dating histories, we hadn't had conversations about our own relationship that I recalled. Our dates were always low key, neither one of us wanting to take whatever we were to the next level. I suppose that is why I felt so safe with him. He moved slowly, which is what I needed to get back into a trusting place, whether he knew that or not.

But now that his ex was in town, my perspective on his taking things slowly swivelled under a different light. Was he being respectful of my feelings, or was he holding back for a different reason?

"HELLO, Daisy. I didn't expect to see you twice in one week," Mr. Stout said as soon as I came through the door.

"Hello Daisy," Ripley squawked from atop a display of boots.

"Hi, Mr. Stout and hello, Ripley. Grandma summoned me," I explained.

Mr. Stout was peeling off the sale stickers from a bin of flip-flops. "I won't keep you then," he said. "Miranda McCartney should not be kept waiting."

I laughed, already several steps up the stairs. "You're right. She is fierce about her schedule." Before I reached the top, the parrot squawked, "Ripley likes donuts. Jimmy like donuts." I wondered what went on in that birdbrain of Ripley's.

Hurrying past Eileen's desk, and shocked to find her sitting there, I said, "May I go in? She just texted."

Eileen flapped her wrist at me. "Go on then," she said. She had a bag of plant food on her desk and was studying the ingredients. I glanced at the window where the dead plant and empty water jug had not budged.

Grandma skipped the formality of chitchat and beckoned me to sit on the couch. As she performed the ethical wall ritual, I noticed a machine on her desk I had never seen before. It was a black contraption, not much bigger than a shoebox with a horizontal line of beads across the side facing me, which turned out to encase tiny little lights.

Before I could ask about it, she started the session in her usual manner. "Now then. What progress have we made this week?"

I stifled a laugh. "Do you mean since yesterday?"

Grandma's feathers did not ruffle easily. She sat stock still in her classic therapist pose and spoke with her classic deadpan therapist voice. "Is that your answer?"

I took a deep breath. "Actually, a lot has happened in one day."

Grandma made a quick nod that encouraged me to elaborate.

"Well, for starters, Jenny fired me, I helped Petra with her new pie making business, I learned Paula is providing foster care for homeless pets, Sadie did in fact visit me at the museum the other night, it is quite possible I have befriended a ghost, dad has apologized for the divorce and encouraged me to 'fill my cup' regardless of whether I choose to study law, oh and Farley was engaged to Sadie and is probably dead. I think. Maybe. I haven't confirmed that last part."

If anything could rattle Miranda McCartney, a few of

the bombs I just dropped would do the trick, but she remained reassuringly placid. "What I am hearing is that you are well on your way to finding your path. Please elaborate on your dead ex-boyfriend."

"I may be on my way to finding some sort of path, but right now it is full of potholes." I drew in a cleansing breath. "Some time after I fell asleep at the security desk the other night, not only did Sadie pay me a visit, of which I have no clear memory, her fiancé who is also my ex, I think, yet to be confirmed by Brett, fell down the stairs and died." I heard my voice waver on that last word and took a breather.

"So Farley is dead," Grandma said. "How does that make you feel?"

"Not great to tell you the truth." I tried. I really did, but maintaining my composure, a skill my grandmother had obviously mastered, was not my forte. Immediately, I dissolved into tears.

Grandma came bounding around the desk, ripped open the pretend curtain, and gathered me into her arms. "Oh honey, I'm so sorry. I know you loved that pompous prick."

She never liked him. He had a swagger she didn't trust. And despite the torrent of emotion spilling out of me, I had my doubts as well. But he cared about me. I know that. Most of my college memories that were any fun included him. He liked to break me out of my rut, over-serve me cosmopolitans, and keep me out all night dancing to alternative rock.

Grandma held me until my tears dried up. Then she brought me a cup of water.

"So you can call people names when you are on the grandma side of the curtain?" I asked, giggling a little.

"Yes," she said. "You needed a good cry. I'm glad I didn't ruin it with my commentary. Are you okay?"

I smiled. It felt like someone had lifted a smallish boulder off me.

"Good." Grandma jumped up, swung the fake curtain closed again and returned to her position behind the desk. "So we can assume for now Farley was back in town to marry this Sadie person and has been prevented from doing so by his own demise. What else?"

"He sent me a letter."

Grandma raised an eyebrow, suggesting I elaborate.

"In retrospect, it was a nice gesture. He wanted to let me know he would be around Lockerbie and that he had moved on. He didn't want things to be awkward."

"A better gesture would have been to tell you in person, but fine. How does Brett feel about this?"

I hung my head. "He doesn't know yet."

Grandma's eyes went wide. "Why not?"

"He told me someone died in the museum. He doesn't know I was working there that night, which likely makes me a suspect. I panicked. Before you jump all over me, I was going to tell him today. I tried to call him on the way over, but he was busy." Opening the "with his ex" can of worms seemed like a topic best tabled for a future session.

"I see. Is there anything else?"

I pointed at the contraption placed between us. "May I ask what is that?"

Grandma's eyes flew to the clock on the wall. Then she huffed. "We don't have time for hypnotherapy, but this is a machine that helps induce a type of hypnotic state."

She turned it on so I could see the beads on the front light up one after another, drawing the eye to the right and back to the left, repeatedly. "Fascinating," I said. "Was this intended for me?"

She shrugged. "I thought it might help you remember

what happened with that Sadie person when you fell asleep at the museum.

"Oh, so the lights would put me in a trance and help me remember? Like retrieve memories I didn't know I had?"

"Not exactly. That sort of mumbo jumbo is fictional. One must be amenable to being hypnotized. Someone can't impose it on you against your will. Think of it as a way to relax your mind enough to think more clearly. The lights enable you to access both sides of your brain."

"Oh, so you can't make me pee my pants or something like that?"

Grandma scoffed. "It's not a slumber party gag, Daisy. But if you open yourself to hypnotism, you are more vulnerable to suggestion."

The door opened, and a shiny faced woman with hot pink hair appeared in the crack. "Sorry," she said.

"Come on in, Cupcake," Grandma said. "Daisy, I'm afraid our session is over. See you Wednesday."

TWELVE

Finally, it was time to get to the museum. I had no books to study, which felt like a relief and a big mistake. However, there was no time to fetch food or books from home, so I bought a cup of noodles from the Mini Mart and headed straight to the museum. If I had any unannounced visitors this evening, I wanted my brain clear and my stomach silent.

I did not notice the police car in the lot behind the museum, which is why I jumped from the shock of finding Brett waiting outside the front doors as I rounded the corner of the house.

"Daisy," he said, his eyes as wide as mine. He was not expecting me either.

"Officer Harnette," I said. He was in his uniform. Was I speaking to an officer who might arrest me or my boyfriend? "Finished with your ex?" I meant that to sound less bitter, but I was rattled. My hands shook as I jammed the key into the door.

He stepped inside and immediately wrapped his arms around me. "I'm sorry," he said into the side of my head.

Feeling the warmth of his breath near my ear calmed me. It felt good to be in his arms. I could have stayed there all night. "It's been a hectic day." He released me and moved his hands to my shoulders. "After she left, I came here to get a copy of the wedding registry for police records. I was just about to text you. Are you working here tonight?"

"Yes, but I am glad I ran into you. I have something to tell you."

SPYING a chesterfield in the living area, Brett led me there. "What is it?" he asked once we were seated. "Are you okay?" He gazed into my eyes, which were still puffy from crying in Grandma's office.

I smiled. "Yes." I wiped the tops of my cheeks, expecting to find chunks of mascara. "I probably look a fright. I had a good cry in therapy today."

Brett's eyes shone with concern.

"I'm fine, really. But I wanted to tell you." I needed to just rip off the band-aid and get it out. Who knew how long I had before his radio would start squawking? "I was working here, in the museum, the other evening. Mom needed me to fill in, but no one came to replace me and I was so tired I fell asleep. When I woke up, I realized I had missed half of my class, so I ran straight to law school."

I drew in an uneven breath. "I wasn't here for a full shift," I continued. "I obviously didn't see whatever happened after I left. I didn't tell you because I am painfully aware my working here that night makes me a suspect if the death was deemed, er, not accidental."

Racing to get it all out, I spoke quickly and stared at my lap. "Was the death accidental?" I asked. I peered up at

Brett, who was still holding my hand. But his mind was elsewhere.

"I don't understand why you didn't tell me," he finally said. "You had at least two opportunities to mention it."

I dropped my gaze. He was right. "I know. I'm sorry. I intended to and then..."

"And then what?"

I inhaled and let the air out slowly, steadying myself. "First, let me ask you. Was the man who died named Farley Shian?"

Brett turned his cheek, staring at some unknown object between us. I could see a muscle in his jaw flex. When he fixed his gaze on me, I felt a blanket of judgment drop. "Yes. Why?"

"Because Farley and I dated for a while in college. And a few days ago, I received a letter from him telling me he was moving back to Lockerbie. He wanted to spare me from feeling awkward about it."

Brett released my hand and stood up. "I don't believe this."

"I know. It's a lot. I'm sorry." I stood up, forcing him to look at me. "You and I have never had that conversation, you know? Where we tell each other the sad stories from our pasts? I wanted to protect that bubble a little longer, I guess."

"You wanted to protect the bubble?" he scoffed. "That is your reason for putting me in this position?"

I expected anger. Maybe disappointment. But I didn't expect to be scolded like a child. "What position?"

"The position where you hold back information important to a case I am working on. The position where I have to decide whether to stay on the case and protect you or reveal my conflict and implicate you in a possible murder case."

Just then, Brett's radio blurted out a coded message requiring his presence. "I've got to go," he said after answering. "Don't tell anyone else until I figure this out. Got it?"

I swallowed. Hard. "Got it."

After he left, I lingered on the couch for a while, wishing I had made different choices.

IT WAS time to give myself a pep talk. I did the right thing. I told Brett what I should have told him days ago. Now it was out of my hands. I did not, in fact, kill anyone, I reminded myself. I had to trust in the process and believe the truth, and my innocence would prevail against whatever odds were stacked up against me.

I wandered into the kitchen and heated my soup with some water. Loitering the halls with a fork in my hand, I ate without tasting. I felt numb, like a zombie haunting the passageways.

Once nourishment set in, my mind churned through recent museum happenings. Farley fell down the stairs. Why was he here? Had someone been here with him? Obviously, I had left. However, someone else was here that night. His fiancée. I stared at the square of rug at the bottom of the stairs, where Farley likely landed.

Why would Sadie come to the museum after it was closed to discuss wedding arrangements? And why could I not remember anything about that conversation? Is it possible she didn't leave? Could she have been here when Farley fell? Maybe she called the police.

Brett needed to know about Sadie. Despite my vague memory, she confirmed she was here at the museum. If the death was not accidental, she should be a suspect, not me.

I texted Brett right away. "Sadie was here the night

Farley died. I don't know when she came or when she left. But she was here."

I drank the last of the liquid from my cup, my conscience now cleared. Then I climbed the stairs, trying to picture the fall, and stopped outside of Riley's room. If his spirit were around, I had not sensed it. Remembering where I was when I may or may not have talked to his ghost, I stepped over the rope again and sat down. How does one summon a ghost?

"Excuse me, Mr. Riley. Are you here?"

His reply came immediately, along with a shiver up my spine. *Where else would I be? You're in my chair.*

I guess that's how.

We started with the pleasantries. He was well, other than being a spirit trapped on Earth. He asked after my family and friends, and I assured him they were all fine. We spent some time discussing Petra's new pie business. He told me his mother made excellent pies from the fruits on their property in Greenfield: apple and peach were his favourites. Rhubarb was his least favourite.

He grew excited when I mentioned Petra's donut rival. His mom made a similar confection from buckwheat every year for his birthday, he told me. Fried cakes with cinnamon were his favourite treat in the world.

We moved to the library where he felt more comfortable being in the company of a lady. We talked about books. He read all the ones in the library while he was alive.When there was a long pause in our conversation, I asked, "So you are real? I thought my imagination gone wild explained our chat."

He chuckled. *A good imagination is a wonderful thing.*

Time flew and my shift was almost over. I wanted to know more about his life. But I was equally keen to know about his more recent observations. "If I may ask, do you pay attention to the events and conversations among the living that take place in this house?"

I suppose I mostly do. I cannot sleep, but I appreciate silence once in a while.

"I imagine this world must feel chaotic for you when compared to simpler times."

I've grown used to it.

"Did you overhear my conversation with Brett? The police officer who was here earlier?" He didn't answer, so I added, "It's okay if you did. I would definitely listen to as many conversations as possible if I couldn't have any of my own."

You are the first with whom I've been able to converse.

"Really? Have you tried talking to others?"

He took some time to answer, and when he did, I caught a sense of weariness in his tone. *I talk to myself constantly and am bored with the company. Believe me, if I could engage anyone, living or dead, in a good chat, I would. But you are apparently the first to see me.*

"That day in the foyer when I woke up. I saw you standing there. I thought it was a dream."

I saw you see me. That is why I worked up the courage to talk to you.

I looked around. "Why can't I see you now?"

I don't know. All I know is there are limits to what I can do in the world where you exist.

"Mr. Riley, I could use your help with something, if you don't mind my asking."

Call me James. And I will if I can.

Wow, what a privilege. "Thank you and please call me Daisy. I'm sorry I never introduced myself. My name is Daisy McCartney."

Pleasure to make your acquaintance Miss... Daisy.

"Um, likewise." Speaking with this man felt like stepping onto a stage and reading lines with an actor. His voice had a forced vernacular that somehow resonated, yet unlike any voice I had encountered. "Okay, so you might have heard a man died in this house a couple of nights ago."

James said nothing, so I pushed on. "Since I was here that night as well, without witnesses, they could accuse me of having something to do with his death."

But you had gone.

I nodded. "I fell asleep, though, before I woke up and saw you. I was late for class, so I ran off. I figured Far.., I mean, the man died after I left. But thank you for confirming I was gone before it happened. That puts my mind at ease."

You are welcome.

"Did you see how he fell? Was it an accident?"

Again, James said nothing.

"If not, I wonder if you saw a woman stop by the museum earlier in the night to see me. I was so tired, I don't remember exactly."

You were sleeping soundly; it is true. I saw the woman. She knocked at the door and when you recognized her; you unlocked it and let her in.

So Sadie was here. "Do you recall any conversation I had with her? Her name is Sadie. She told me today she wanted to ask about wedding stuff that the museum provides services for. Do you know if we talked about anything else?"

I recall little of the conversation; I am sorry to say. You let her in. She talked to you in a low voice. And then you were asleep again.

What? "I fell asleep while she was talking to me?"

That is what it looked like to me.

Interesting. "That was rude of me. Did I wake up to let her out? Or did she leave on her own?"

On that, I cannot be sure. Once you were asleep, I lost interest. Conversations I find interesting. But I rarely follow people around and watch what they do.

"So you went to your room and rested?"

Yes.

"When the man fell down the stairs, did you see anything, then?"

Again, James didn't reply. Was he unwilling to comment on how or when Farley died? "You don't want to talk about it, do you?"

It is bad luck to speak of the dead.

"I see." I wondered if he was the only ghost lurking in the house. "Is anyone here with you?"

I have never met a ghost besides myself, if that's what you are asking.

"It must be lonely."

You have no idea.

"Well, thank you for answering my questions."

I hope it helped.

"If you can tell me anything else about that night after I left and before the man died, I would appreciate it."

No response.

"I wonder why I am the only one who can talk to you and why you are the only ghost I can hear," I mused out loud.

I have wondered the same. There must be some divine purpose, but I don't know what.

THIRTEEN

Brett never replied to my text. I supposed he was wrapped up in police business. Or he was mad at me.

On my walk home, I kept my eyes peeled for anyone who might follow me. Petra's suspicions about Stan had me paranoid. But the walk was uneventful. I saw no shadowy figures trailing behind me or ducking into bushes.

When I returned home, a small sheep greeted me. At least, that was the best way to describe the ball of fluff that yipped and offered me a paw. She was sheep sized with matted terry cloth fur. I could hear Paula snoring as the dog followed me upstairs. Craving company, I let her jump into bed with me. Since Paula now sheltered needy animals, I could do my part, making them feel comfortable.

The mail Paula mentioned earlier, a handwritten letter with no return address, was on my desk. With the dog snuggled up beside me, I read the letter by the light of my bedside table lamp. I read every word twice. Then I sent Brett another text:

"You should know I received another letter from Farley. You will want to see this. Meet me at Pie Latte (formerly

Petra's Pastries) tomorrow?" The letter's contents would have kept me awake were it not for the little snorts and quivers from Sheba. Her steadfast heartbeat soothed me to sleep.

WHEN I AWOKE, my wooly buddy was gone. I immediately checked my phone. No word from Brett, but Paula had texted me. "Taking Sheba for a walk. Can you come to St. Jo's Brewery tonight for drinks? Rita and Petra will be there."

That sounded fun. I immediately replied yes, then tried not to obsess over Brett's silence. His failure to reply to my urgent texts was worrisome, but I assumed he was busy. If he was mad at me, I did not want to know.

I brought the letter to show Petra. I hoped she could give me some reassurance. But before I arrived at Pie Latte, she texted me.

HAVE YOU SEEN THE NEWS?

"What news?"

They found your ex dead at the JWR museum.

Oh right. I hadn't told her.

Did you know about this?!

"Yes, but not confirmed until last night. Please, just tell me if the news says how he died?" Please say accidental, please say accidental, please say accidental...

He fell down the stairs.

. . .

THERE WAS no time for chitchat once I got to Pie Latte. The line out the door was longer than yesterday's. A fresh group of students were busy churning out, boxing up and selling pies. I found Petra cutting pie dough with dozens of foil pie pans stacked around her. She handed me recipes and sent me to the kitchen to work on pie fillings.

Before she rushed away, I asked, "Did he fall or was he pushed?" She wrinkled her forehead in confusion and shoved me toward the stove. The next time she appeared in my part of the kitchen, she said, "I would have pushed him," which didn't help at all.

Meanwhile, I checked my phone every chance I could for a message from Brett. Nothing. Paula, on the other hand, contacted me. After repeatedly calling and getting my voicemail, she texted, "Did you hear about Farley? Funeral is tomorrow." Somehow, I had not considered the inevitable funeral.

Hours later, Petra ran out of supplies. She had to hurry to make it to a class she was teaching. "I'll see you tonight," she said on her way out, leaving a leftover piece of pie and latte in her wake.

"Thank you!" I shouted at her disappearing backside. The pie was delicious: Kentucky bourbon pecan. I do not know what the latte was called, but it tasted like Thanksgiving.

I had Farley's letter in my pocket, but no word from Brett. Since I was still a law student, I went to class. Paula and Rita would be at the museum running tours. Dad would be doing the thing he does best at his law firm. With no salon job, law school was the only distraction I had left.

You would think Professor Mango would be pleased to see me arriving early for class. I even raised my hand and answered one question — correctly, I should add, by some miracle. He raised an eyebrow in surprise. Even with that small encouragement, I was feeling noncommittal about law school. Part of me wanted to stay and part of me did not. The freedom to acknowledge my ambivalence felt better than knowing all the answers. Perhaps it was okay to feel two things at once.

After class, Tad appeared at my locker. "It's almost like you studied," he joked, referencing the question I answered in class. With my phone still eerily silent, I agreed to join him for coffee in the lounge.

Farley was all over the news. We watched highlights on the lounge TV until I felt queasy.

"Are you okay?" Tad asked. "You haven't touched your coffee."

I levelled with him. "Farley Shian was my ex-boyfriend." There. I said it.

Tad's jaw dropped open. "Oh geez. I'm sorry." The concern in his expression felt authentic. How sweet. "Unless you are not sorry?" he said.

I sighed. "There was no bad blood, if that's what you mean. Baggage, maybe. Fodder for therapy. But we weren't enemies."

He eyed me over the rim of his cup. "That's good. Nothing worse than a bad breakup. Do you know the fiancée?" He tilted his head at the TV, where reporters were questioning Sadie outside Dixie Donuts.

"We recently met." I didn't want to dwell on that topic longer than I had to.

The transcription across the bottom of the screen reported Sadie's shock and sadness over her foiled wedding plans. Reporters asked if she would take over the business since the elder Shians had recently announced plans to retire. Sadie said no, they had not advised her what would happen to the business.

"Her hair is mesmerizing, isn't it?" Tad said. Sadie was sporting her signature side nobs.

"Yes, it's hard to look away when she talks," I said, but Tad didn't seem to hear me. I narrowed my eyes. He was completely rapt. As the camera zoned in on Sadie talking, I watched his eyes move back and forth, from one blond nob to the other.

"Holy donut holes, that's it!" I said.

"Huh?" Tad was still transfixed.

"I have to go," I told him.

I bolted out the door and ran all the way to Grandma's office. It was getting close to 5:00 when I knew she would wrap up with the last patient of the day.

Stopping at Eileen's desk, because she was actually there, I asked if I could go in. "Of course," she said, just as Grandma and a woman emerged from the office. The client wailed and mumbled incoherently all the way to the door and down the steps. I raised my eyebrows questioningly at Grandma, who simply shrugged. "I'm afraid we're out of time," she said to no one in particular.

"Grandma," I said. "Sorry to barge in, but I have to ask you something. Can you give me a minute?"

She huffed. "Fine, but you're buying me a drink after." I smiled, wondering if Paula deserved another figurative gold star. Had she invited Grandma to the brewery?

Once inside, I told her about what happened with Tad and the TV. Then I recounted what happened whenever I seemed to interact with Sadie. "It's like the machine you have," I said. "She uses her eyes, and those hair nobs, and I don't know what else to keep our eyes moving. Is it possible she is hypnotizing people when she does that?"

Grandma sat at her desk, pondering for a moment. "I suppose so. You'd have to be amenable to letting it happen. Remember, you can't be hypnotized against your will."

"Right," I said. "But if you didn't know it was happening, and she knew how to do that power of suggestion thing, is it possible you could kind of fall under her spell?"

She laughed. "It's not witchcraft, Daisy-doo." She saw my disappointed reaction and asked, "Why? What are you worried about?"

I was worried Sadie had lulled me to sleep so she could knock off her rich fiancé.

WE FOUND PETRA, Paula and Rita at the bar, slinging back Confessional IPAs.

"You brought Miranda," Mom exclaimed, a little too enthusiastically.

"Be nice," I whispered as I kissed her on the cheek.

"Hello, Paula," Grandma said. "Long time no see."

Petra slid over a couple of stools so Grandma could sit by Rita, who struck up a conversation with Grandma about repetitive behaviour.

"Remind me why we stopped going to the pub," Petra asked me. She preferred sipping Scotch at Lockerbie Pub to craft beer tasting.

"Something to do with me almost getting murdered there?" I said. "I could be wrong."

Petra grinned, shaking her head. "You're going to keep playing that card until the day you *die*, aren't you?"

"Ha, ha," I said sarcastically, "Even if it kills me." We ordered our drinks, and even though I missed drinking cosmopolitans, I admit the stout was growing on me. It tasted like chocolate and coffee. "Hey, thank you for the pie today."

"No problem. Did you like the latte?"

"I did. What makes it taste like Thanksgiving?"

"It's a mix of pecan pie and pumpkin flavours — it wasn't easy to get right," Petra said.

I glanced at the others, who were deep in conversation about what food to order. "Petra," I said in a low voice. "I'm desperate to talk to you about something. I received a *letter from the dead,* if you get my drift."

Our beers arrived and Petra scowled at me as she sipped her Tangerine Wit. "I do not get your drift," she said after she swallowed.

"Farley wrote me a second letter," I whispered. "It arrived Wednesday, but I didn't have time to read it until last night."

Petra set her beer glass down on the lacquered wooden table. Now I had her attention. "What did it say?"

I patted my pocket. "I have it here, but," I looked to confirm the others were still distracted, "the gist is he thought someone was trying to kill him, he was in trouble or in debt or something, and he wanted me to know he had changed the beneficiary on his life insurance from Sadie to me." Saying it aloud did nothing to ease the queasiness in my gut as I had hoped. Was Farley trying to reach out to me for help? I could never ask him now.

"He didn't!"

"He did," I said. "He attached the policy."

"But why?" Petra asked.

I shrugged. "Who knows? Maybe he wanted to protect Sadie somehow."

"And put *you* in danger?"

I chewed on the side of my cheek. "I know. It's not good

for me either way. Not only will I have Sadie, and whoever is after him, as an enemy, but guess who now has an incentive to want him dead?"

Petra slumped over her beer. "The person who was at the scene of the crime the night he died."

"Bingo," I said.

"You two are thick as thieves over there," Paula shouted to us across the others.

"Sorry," I said. "Who's hungry? Do we have a food plan?"

Petra and I picked up our menus as the others made suggestions. I whispered to Petra as I scanned the happy hour specials, "I need advice. ASAP."

Petra pretended to consider the menu selections, but her eyes were wide as if she had seen a ghost.

FOURTEEN

Seeing Mr. and Mrs. Shian for the first time since their son and I broke up was disturbing enough. Seeing them at Farley's funeral brought painfully awkward to a new level. They had always been charitable and upbeat. Now their shoulders slumped with the weight of their grief.

Paula and I had barely spoken during the hour drive to Bloomington. She sampled one too many of the artisan beers last night and kept nodding off. I used the quiet time to think; trying to work out how to save my bacon.

The radio silence from Brett had me feeling unsettled. He was likely disappointed in me, while also trying to clear my name and juggling other police business. Given the information I held back from him for so long, I couldn't blame him for keeping his distance.

The closer we got to the funeral home, the more agitated and jumpy I felt. Every nerve prickled with the expectation of sirens blaring toward me any second.

My flimsy plan was to talk to as many people as possible at the funeral and hope that a clue or two would drop in my lap. Something that would point the finger away from me.

Worst case, I would loudly accuse Sadie of hypnotizing me. Maybe she would snap and let slip some key piece of information.

Chief among my concerns, and I admit my experience with Jolee's death had me paranoid on this point, was that Farley didn't fall at all but was killed some other sneaky way, then moved to the bottom of the stairs.

Thanks to Brett, I knew Farley was eating a donut that night. What if someone poisoned the donut with something the police couldn't detect? Until I heard from Brett about the test results on that donut, no dead body was going into any hole at this funeral if I could prevent it.

My heart ached for the Shians, who lost their only son. "No one should outlive their children," they commented when I expressed my condolences. As they hugged me and thanked me for coming, I wondered if they would sell their business or let Sadie run it. The question felt too inappropriate to ask.

Sadie, I noticed, was working the room. She wore a shiny black skirt and matching blouse. On her lapel gleamed a pink jewelled brooch shaped like a donut. She wore her hair in loose curls tucked behind her ears. I wondered if anyone else noticed the mismatched earrings: one was a miniature version of the brooch; the other an emerald studded star.

I spotted Stan among the attendees. Wearing a navy suit, he hung back in a corner of the room clutching his bowling bag. Since he looked as out of place as I felt, I walked over to say hello.

"It was thoughtful of you to come, Stan."

"Least I could do," he said. "I know he meant something to you once." When I tilted my head in confusion, he added, "Paula told me."

Remembering the blue jug he had when I last saw him, I asked about his psoriasis. He assured me the pain was well managed. "Surprising how many antifreeze containers they throw out behind Dixie Donuts," he said.

"Antifreeze?" I asked.

"Yes. There are always more of those containers when I check the alley. I've been collecting them for recycling. People don't always think to sort trash," he said.

"I guess not." I tried to act cool, but my mind was spinning. Doesn't antifreeze kill pets if they eat it? A certain veterinarian I once knew mentioned that antifreeze kills dozens of pets each year because the stuff tastes so sweet. Could people detect it? I wondered.

I was lost in thought when Sadie approached us. "Thank you for coming," she said, her voice flat.

"Of course," I replied.

When she thanked Stan, he explained Lockerbie's plastic recycling options.

I did not detect any defensiveness in Sadie over Stan's reference to irresponsible trash sorting outside the donut shop. But I noticed Stan's eyes darting from one of her ears to the other. Speaking in that soft tone used by yoga and kindergarten teachers, Sadie winked and suggested that Stan keep her recycling missteps under his hat.

"Say, Sadie." I butted in more loudly than intended, interrupting her conversation with Stan. She swung around, surprised to see I was still there, perhaps. I fixed my eyes upon her brooch. I know Grandma said hypnotism requires willingness, but I wasn't taking any chances. "I don't know what to do about something," I said to the brooch. "But maybe you can help. I received a strange letter from Farley."

"Yes," she said. "He was so thoughtful to let you know about our relationship. I hope it didn't cause you any hurt feelings." So she knew. Why hadn't she mentioned it when I talked to her before?

"Right. Thoughtful," I said to the brooch. "I was happy to know he found someone. But I am not referring to the first letter. It's the second one I thought you should know about. The one that arrived after he died."

"Oh?"

Judging by her tone, she didn't know about that one. In the corner of my eye, I saw Stan snap out of his trance as I mentioned the letter. This was good. I could use a witness right now. "I wonder if you might advise me. He was sure someone was trying to kill him. I don't understand the reasoning. Maybe you can enlighten me, but he amended his life insurance to make me his beneficiary. Any idea why he would do that?"

I was studiously avoiding her face, steering clear of those mesmerizing earrings. However, even in periphery I could not miss the horrified reaction on her face or the shudder in her shoulder.

"I am sure you are mistaken," she finally said. "I have the policy in a safe at home. I can assure you the beneficiary has not changed."

"Oh, that's a relief," I said. "Because the version he sent me was signed the day before his death, witnessed and notarized." I paused for effect, still gazing at that stupid brooch. "Speaking as a lowly law student, and I am no notary expert, it sure looked like he dotted all the i's and crossed all the t's."

I peered at Stan, whose face seemed to register a previously calm Sadie becoming more and more rattled. Glancing at the bowling bag clutched in his hand, I noticed it was partially unzipped. Inside I spotted something mechanical with a blinking light, but I could not be sure. Besides, I needed to keep my attention on Sadie.

"That's interesting," Sadie finally said. "Do you have the policy with you? Perhaps I could have the company's lawyer take a look at it." She pointed to a portly fellow in a charcoal suit across the room who was talking to the Shians.

"Oh, could you?" I said. "I don't want to be any trouble. But I would feel so much better knowing you would be well cared for, as Farley must have intended."

I reached into my purse and gave her a copy of the original from Farley's letter. Stan and I watched her walked toward the Shians, then veer last minute into the hallway.

"It's not the original, is it?" Stan said to me.

"No, but it doesn't matter. The insurance company would have the updated version. I just wanted to see what she would do."

"Personally, I would have gone with the poisoning angle," Stan said.

I raised my chin and gave him a respectful nod. "The antifreeze? Impressive sleuthing, Stan."

"Thanks. I've been meaning to apologize to you."

I laughed. "For what?" I glanced at the door, curious about what Sadie was doing exactly.

"I know I've been hovering a lot," Stan replied, studying his shoes sheepishly.

I raised an eyebrow. "You have been tailing me, haven't you? Petra thought you were."

"Yes, but I'm no stalker."

"Well, I wouldn't use the word..."

"Just a little overprotective," Stan continued. "But I managed to get Sadie on video when you let her in the museum that night. Before you fell asleep. She asked Farley to wait outside and she gave him a donut to make him happy. It looked like the same type my hidden camera caught her injecting with antifreeze earlier that day."

I gasped. "You didn't."

"I did."

My gleeful giggle turned quickly to a disappointed groan. "It's probably not admissible."

"I suspect your dad will think of something if it comes to that," Stan said with a gleam in his eye.

AFTER THE FUNERAL, I hitched a ride home with Petra. Stan, eager to talk about book club marketing points with Paula, convinced her to let him drive her home.

"She really tried to burn the document in the bathroom?" Petra said, after we shared a good belly laugh.

"She did. That's why the sprinklers went off."

"That's just priceless. Definitely worth ruining my funeral dress for." Still laughing, she took another towel from the stack between us and dried her eyes.

"I'll buy you another with all my insurance money," I said.

"You're keeping it?" I couldn't tell if Petra was surprised or appalled.

"No," I admitted. "It will probably become part of the evidence for the trial. Whoever gets that money won't have access to it for a while."

"Too bad," Petra said.

"Why? I can still replace the dress. I have some pie money coming in."

"Ha, speaking of my business. I have a proposition for you."

"Oh, do tell," I said.

"I found some property on the other side of Lockerbie,

as far as I could get from Dixie Donuts and still be in Lockerbie."

"You're buying a place?"

"Yes. I've been saving for a while and this opportunity came along at just the right time."

"Good for you!"

"There's an extra room, with a full bath and everything," she said.

"Can I rent it from you?" I blurted. Now I was excited.

"Oh, I'm so glad you asked. Yes! I know things with Paula can get a little intense. You would have the whole half of the upstairs to yourself. I'll be on the other half, but it will be like having your own apartment."

"Sounds perfect, Petra, thank you!"

"There is a catch."

"Oh, okay. Is this why you hoped I'd be keeping the insurance? How much? I'll borrow from Dad if I have to. Quit law school even..."

"No, not that. I want to move Pie Latte to the storefront downstairs. It's a commercial property, actually. Mixed use. There's a space that is perfect for pie making and it has a great kitchen. I was hoping you'd be my pie partner as well as my tenant."

"Petra, if you weren't driving right now, I would hug the Charles Dickens out of you. Yes, yes, yes! Until I started helping, I did not know much fun pie making could be. To make pies with you means I won't have to hunt you down every time there's something exciting to tell you, and..."

"Okay, I get it. Your answer is yes. You're welcome."

I sat quietly for a moment, letting this news sink in. I didn't want to over enthuse. She might change her mind once she pictures me nattering at her all day. But then I heard a sniffle. "Petra, are you okay?"

"Yes," she said, swiping at her nose. "It's not like I'm having a good day or anything. Just allergies."

"Right."

"You probably gave me a cold, making those sprinklers go off."

"Yep. All my fault."

For the first time since Jolee died, I felt a clearer sense of purpose. Perhaps her death closed a window on my hair styling aspirations. Perhaps Petra's offer opened a door to something new. All I knew was that I was excited about this new direction, and I could not stop beaming at Petra as we drove back to Lockerbie.

Eventually, she told me to stop 'creeping her out.' So I focused on the road ahead and changed the subject. "How about I tell you a ghost story?"

FIFTEEN

Back at home, Paula made an announcement. "Sheba is not just a foster pet," she said, handing Petra and me glasses of champagne. "She's mine. I completed the adoption today."

"Congratulations!" Petra said, as we clinked our glasses.

"Cheers, Mom!" I took a sip before hugging her. "You have certainly earned it. I cannot think of a more deserving dog mom."

We sat in the tiny parlour where we used to host book club meetings. Sheba was curled up at Paula's feet. We were all tired. It had been an eventful day.

So much had changed in the past few months. Mom had busied herself organizing the new version of the Penny Lane Book Club now that the stick house renovation that occupied both of us for so many years was done. Now Sheba was here to keep Mom company. I looked forward to the next stage in my life: pie making with Petra and whatever else came my way.

"You are becoming quite the crime solver," Mom said, interrupting my reverie.

"Oh," I said. "I don't know about that. Perhaps I am just gifted at being in the wrong place at the right time."

Petra laughed and clinked her glass against mine. "Amen to that!"

But Mom seemed less amused. "I mean it, Daisy. You have a good head on your shoulders." She reached down and stroked Sheba's back. "I am proud of you."

PAULA WENT TO BED EARLY. Between the drinks last night and the funeral mayhem, she could barely drag herself up the stairs.

Sheba and I walked Petra home. As we strolled through the neighbourhood and introduced Sheba to the dog friendly gardens along the way, I felt a sense of peace. Though Paula did not know about my plan to move out, I knew Sheba would soften the blow, smoothing the transition for her. Not that Mom would ever dissuade me from spreading my wings. We both knew I wouldn't live on Penny Lane forever. I wouldn't be far away, and Sheba would fill Paula's home with love and purpose.

Back at home, I led Sheba to her doggie bed next to Paula, kissed her fluffy head, and slipped out the door. There was one more thing I had to do.

I WALKED around the corner to the museum, unlocked the door, and stepped inside.

"James?" I called.

In here, he said. I followed his voice into the library and sat on a wing-backed chair.

You are here late. Even the security desk person went home.

"I know. I wanted to tell you what happened today."

I told him all about the funeral, Sadie's involvement in Farley's death, and how relieved I felt now that I was not a suspect. Throughout my rambling account, James stayed quiet. I suppose when you are dead; you become a better listener.

"So," I concluded. "It looks like she poisoned him. Maybe she pushed him down the stairs. Maybe he fell. Either way, the poison would have got him."

Finally, James broke the silence. *Perhaps I should not have pushed him then.*

"What?" Did I hear that right?

Now it was James's time to talk.

He was eating a donut. I could not take the smell, Daisy. Moreover, before you ask, I cannot usually cause objects to move. However, if I am angry or especially worked up about something, strange things can happen.

I did not mean to push him or cause him to stumble. I wanted him to take the donut somewhere else. It is pure torment for me to smell them and not be able to eat them, or to be with my mother when she would ask about my birthday wishes. I fear that all of my emotional energy collided with Farley that night.

"Wow. I could have used that information a little sooner." I heard a rumble of laughter from James at that. It was the sort of laugh that comes from relief; from working through something with another person.

How are things with your gentleman friend?

"Brett? Oh, we'll be fine. He has a major embezzlement case right now. He apologized for not being around much. I think we will be okay." This I knew from a few harried texts he finally sent. We had yet to talk about the Farley murder case. We had yet to get into any sort of relationship discussion. For now, I would pull a Scarlet O'Hara on those thoughts.

Do me a favour, will you, Daisy?

Anything.

If you love him, do not wait to be with him. Pursue your dreams, yes, but try to include him in them. Do not get to the end of your life wishing you had committed to love before it was too late.

"Hmm, wise words. Almost as if you are speaking from experience."

I wonder, Daisy, if this was my purpose. To share a bit of my heartbreak to spare you from making my mistakes.

I must have drifted off, because suddenly my eyelids flew open. I was still in the museum's library and I could see the morning light brightening the hallway. "James? Are you still there? I think I fell asleep." But I already knew he was gone.

EPILOGUE

"Thank you for gathering here today on such short notice," Paula said. We were standing in the reception hall behind the museum. Paula and Rita negotiated free space for the Penny Lane Book Club to meet on one Sunday evening each month. Apparently, few events occurred on Sunday nights, and because Paula, Rita and I worked there, we could save the museum from hiring people to set up chairs, serve refreshments and clean up afterwards.

"Before we hear updates from the marketing spokespersons," she nodded at Stan and Karen, who had teamed up to compile and report on the survey information, "I want to express my appreciation to all of you. Books are important. They inform us, reflect our inner struggles, bond us together, and enable us to escape now and then from," she gave me a small sympathetic smile, "loss, life and turmoil."

Next, Paula singled out the individuals who volunteered for committees set up to explore charitable pursuits, food and wine, book selection guidelines, and other subjects important to the group members. Unlike the museum, the reception hall had modern conveniences like a large kitchen, roomy bathrooms, and space to accommodate crowds.

After the reports, we selected our first book, Lucy Foley's *The Guest List*. The library committee passed out hard copies and arranged for ebook and audiobook sharing to accommodate everyone.

Then we stood around and chatted, holding glasses of wine donated by The Lockerbie Pub and plates of savoury mini scones contributed by Petra.

"I thought you weren't making scones anymore," I said to my friend and soon-to-be business partner.

"Not for profit," she said. "For fun." Petra's baking interests had widened since she closed Petra's Pastries officially, and started experimenting again. She seemed to smile more lately, I noticed — and quoted Sartre, who I found depressing, less.

"You seem happier," I said.

"Happiness is like a butterfly; the more you chase it, the more it will elude you," Petra said.

"That doesn't sound like Sartre."

She smiled. "There's more. 'But if you turn your attention to other things, it will come and sit softly on your shoulder.'"

"Whoever said that was wise," I said.

"Henry David Thorough," she informed me. "I think his words apply to you as well. You know, with how you explore your various interests."

I laughed. "I think you just called me flaky."

Someone tapped me on my shoulder. Probably Stan, I thought, as I turned to find Brett, dressed in jeans and a flannel shirt. "Wow," I said, as he kissed my cheek. "You aren't working tonight?"

He held up a copy of the book club book. "Had to come

get my book," he said. "And to apologize to my girlfriend for ignoring her so much lately."

That was the first time he had used the word girlfriend. I liked the way it sounded. It was unfortunate my hands were full because I felt an urge to hug him and get a real kiss. I scanned quickly for a nearby table to set down my glass and plate, but before I located one, Stan appeared. "Officer Harnette," he said. "I wanted to ask you some questions about the Shian case."

Brett shook Stan's hand, placing his free hand gently on Stan's arm. "Another time?" He glanced at me. "I'm trying to make up with my girlfriend here."

Stan, who was not holding his bowling bag tonight, put both hands in his pockets and dipped his head. "Sorry. I understand."

He looked so lost and disappointed; I wanted to rescue him. "Actually, I have some questions, too. If you really want to make it up to me..."

Brett raised his hands in a U shape above his shoulders, surrendering. "Fine. Between the four of us, though? If any of you breathe a word, I will deny everything."

Petra, Stan and I leaned closer. "We won't tell anyone, right Petra? Stan?" I said.

Brett narrowed his eyes and made us pinky swear. After we locked pinky fingers with his, he continued. "Okay, you know the embezzlement case that has been keeping me so busy?"

I rolled my eyes and nodded.

"It relates to a certain donut enterprise in town. We got a tip from an insider. It seems Farley found out about it and was going to blow the whistle."

"Who was embezzling? They must have been scary people if Farley thought they might kill him." I said.

"She doesn't look that scary, but I wouldn't put it past her." Brett said with a wink.

"She might even poison a donut," Stan said, with the air of someone who knew more than he should.

"Thanks for turning over your evidence," Brett said to Stan. "Without it, we might not have been able to connect her to the embezzlement case." He turned to explain to Petra and I. "Once Sadie realized we were looking at her for murder, she tried to play the sympathy card. She only started embezzling because Farley refused to take over the company from his parents. He wanted to start a skydiving company instead."

"Skydiving?" I said. "I didn't know he was into thrill seeking."

"Neither did Sadie," Brett said. "But she didn't want to marry a broke sky diver. She wanted to marry a wealthy corporate owner. When my source told Farley about the disappearing funds being linked to Sadie, he advised Farley to move some assets to protect the company from bankruptcy. But Farley must have had bigger worries about Sadie's intentions, since changing the beneficiary of his life insurance policy was the first thing he did."

I gasped. "Will Dixie Donuts go bankrupt?" I thought about the Shians. They did not deserve to have their life's work go up in flames.

"Hopefully not. That part of the embezzlement case is confidential." Brett made his voice serious and low. "Remember; don't breathe a word about this to anyone. Tracking the funds will be more complicated if certain people find out about what we are investigating."

I had so many questions. We all did. But Brett's information tap shut down just as I saw Tad walking toward our group.

"Hi, Daisy." Petra took a couple of steps back so Tad could join the conversation.

"Tad!" He was the last person I expected to see at the book club meeting. "Are you joining the book club?"

He held up his library card. "Just got my audio download today," he said.

Brett cleared his throat next to me.

"Excuse me," Petra said, and scampered off.

"Sorry." I watched Petra leave, who I knew was not fond of awkward situations. She could read my unease like a book. "Brett, Stan, this is Tad, my law school friend. Tad, this is..."

Brett thrusted out his hand. "I'm her boyfriend, Officer Harnette."

That seemed aggressive, I thought. Now that I saw Tad standing there, shaking hands with Brett, his eyes darting to mine for help, I remembered something.

"Actually, Brett and Stan, would you excuse us for a minute?" Before they could answer, I grabbed Tad's arm and steered him to the refreshments table. "Would you like a scone?" I asked. "Or wine?"

"No," he said. "Thank you. What was that?" He gestured to the place we had been standing, where Brett was surveying us with steely eyes.

"I don't know. He rarely acts so territorial. But listen, I wanted to ask you, and I hope this doesn't sound weird, but did you put something in my locker?"

"Oh," Tad said, suddenly interested in a platter of scones. "Yeah, I didn't know you have a boyfriend."

I sighed. "That's very sweet. I enjoyed the note, really. It's one of my favourite Riley quotes."

Tad visibly relaxed, his shoulders dropping away from his ears. "Oh good. I thought that maybe we could... But now I know we couldn't..." His eyes darted to the section of the room where Brett stood again. "I didn't know."

I laughed. "It's okay. I'm not sure I knew either until tonight."

He nodded. "Well, I'm going to get started on the book," he said. "See you next month!"

As Tad scurried out of the room, I took in the surrounding crowd: neighbours, strangers and friends clumped together in small groups, talking and laughing.

Tragedy had struck twice in Lockerbie over the past several months. Now that we had a book club again, I felt that maybe the tide was turning. Making my way back to Brett, who was already headed toward me, I uttered a quiet prayer for the health and safety of everyone in the room.

SALTED CARAMEL PEANUT BUTTER DONUTS

Ingredients

- 2/3 C.flour
- 1/3 C. peanut butter powder (like PB&Me)
- 1/4 tsp. baking soda
- 1/4 tsp. salt
- 1/3 C. sugar
- 1/2 C. almond milk (or any type of milk)
- 1 tsp. apple cider vinegar
- 2 tbsp. butter (melted and cooled)
- 1/4 C. creamy peanut butter
- 1 tsp. vanilla extract

Salted Caramel Frosting

- 2 tbsp. butter
- 1/2 C. brown sugar
- 3 tbsp. milk
- 3/4 C. powdered sugar, sifted
- 1/2 tsp. vanilla extract

- Sea salt flakes, to taste

Instructions

1. Preheat oven to 375 F. and grease a donut pan.
2. In a large bowl, whisk together all the dry ingredients.
3. In another bowl, stir together wet ingredients until combined.
4. Pour wet ingredients into dry and mix until just combined (don't over-mix).
5. Spoon mixture into donut moulds, smoothing out the top of the batter for each donut.
6. Bake 10-12 minutes or until a toothpick comes out clean. Allow donuts to cool completely before frosting.

Frosting

1. Melt butter in a saucepan over medium heat. Stir in brown sugar and 3 tbsp. of milk. Boil vigorously for one minute.
2. Remove from heat and stir in 1/2 C. of powdered sugar. Cool slightly, then beat in vanilla and remaining 1/4 C. of powdered sugar. Add more milk or sugar for desired consistency. Then spread frosting over each donut. Sprinkle with sea salt.

EXCERPT FROM SCONE COLD MURDER

CHAPTER 1

6 AM THURSDAY, SEPTEMBER 16

Jolee Lennon was face down just inside Kensington Park.

Petra found her at 5:15 in the morning after baking several dozen scones at her coffee shop, Petra's Pastry Café. She had to walk from one corner of Lockerbie Square to the opposite corner where she rents the top floor of a restored Victorian mansion called the Foote House.

The Kensington Park garden is just behind a gate that is unlocked sporadically by a groundskeeper. This morning, as Petra passed the Park she found the gate open, prompting her to step inside and reflect on her life choices. (Why she had not delegated the 3 AM scone making to one of her students, for example.)

She was now recounting these details (not the life choices part, she told me that later) to the officer at the scene. Mom and I were staring at the body's sprawled out backside. Jolee's purple-tipped blond locks were uncharacteristically askew, her dress was hiked up too high (it was the polka dotted dress she'd worn to the Salon the previous day), and she was laying face-down on the grass by a flowering shrub.

"I found her and called 911 right away," Petra explained, before pointing at me. "Then I texted Daisy."

The police officer cocked his head at me, a not-quite-smile at the corner of his smooth-shaven mouth. "You always awake at," he glanced at the notebook in his hand, "five in the morning, Miss...?"

"McCartney," I told him. "Daisy McCartney. And yes. Petra knows I study off and on all night." My body wanted to squirm under his appraising stare. His eyes, brown and serious, appealed to the wrong side of me. The side I try to keep under wraps, lest I lose my footing and trip over my heart. "I'm always up late studying," I added. His chocolate eyes searched mine, which made me nervous. I ramble when I'm nervous. "I work all day at Jolee's Salon. And I go to law school at night. Hence, the late night studying." I half expected Jolee to lift her head and explain the rest. *She works too hard, this girl.* Jo would say. *I don't know how you do it, Daisy. Don't you want a social life?* "You're all the social I can handle," I'd tell her.

"I see," said the officer. "And how do you know Ms. Lennon?" He glanced at Petra, who was staring at the body, shaking her head.

"She's a good friend," I said, meeting his eyes and feeling a lurch in my stomach. I watched Petra walk over to the fountain, pausing in front of the trickle of water spewing over itself into the basin. "We met at book club. She doesn't go anymore," I added, thinking back to the early meetings, when I had time to kill.

"And how do you two know each other?" he asked, nodding over at Petra. "She teaches near the law school. Sometimes I catch a ride." And she's the best friend I have left, I didn't add.

"I don't understand," Mom interrupted, gesturing to Jolee's backside. "How did she die? She was just at my house a few hours ago." Her eyes scanned Jolee's body like she might find an encoded answer there. "She was fine. She was…" Mom's voice trailed off. She and I both knew Jolee was not fine.

AFTERWORD

I hope you enjoyed reading this book as much as I did writing it. Please take a moment to leave a review wherever you purchased DONUT ENTER.

If you want to be the first to know about Book 3, NEVER SAY PIE, and other exciting news, consider "buying me a coffee" at https://www.buymeacoffee.com/maryanntip !

ACKNOWLEDGMENTS

A big thank you to the real life James Whitcomb Riley Museum staff, especially the knowledgable young woman who led our tour of the mansion in July 2022 when I visited with my sister and stepmom. Thank you for providing such interesting anecdotes and for not questioning the eight million pictures I took of the home's layout.

The writing community on Instagram is filled with amazing people. Several kind volunteers read a draft of this book and gave me valuable feedback. Thank you, Heather Thornton, Megan Lassek, Kirsty L. Ghostly, Julia Kautz, and Leslie Mondle for your kind-hearted contributions to the final version.

Thank you, Alan, for trying not to talk to me while I wrote the first draft and for proofreading the final one. Doing life with you is such fun.

To all my friends, who ask me about my writing and say supportive things when I talk about a little community in Indianapolis where fictitious murders keep happening, thank you for caring. You know who you are.

Most of all, thank you, reader, for picking up this book. You took the time to read my story, and for that I am forever grateful.

ABOUT THE AUTHOR

Mary Ann Tippett writes uplifting fiction from her home in Ottawa. She enjoys long walks, listening to Beatles music and attending monthly book club meetings (where no members have been murdered). *DoNut Enter* is her second cozy mystery in the Penny Lane Book Club Mystery series.

www.ingramcontent.com/pod-product-compliance
Lightning Source LLC
Chambersburg PA
CBHW020140150626
46552CB00021B/846